CW00525540

Séduction

THE SCARLET LIBRARY
LONDON MMI

THE SCARLET LIBRARY

is an imprint of
THE *Erotic* Print Society
EPS, 1 Maddox Street
LONDON W1S 2PZ

Tel (UK only): 0800 026 25 24
Fax: +44 (0)20 7437 3528
Email: *eros@eps.org.uk*
Web: *www.scarletlibrary.com*
OR *www.eroticprints.org*

ISBN: 1-898998-32-9

© 2001 MacHo Ltd, London UK

Séduction

ANONYMOUS

translated by
Jeremy Leah

with new
illustrations by

SYLVIE JONES

THE SCARLET LIBRARY

CONTENTS

THE BOOK

This translation of *Séduction (Jeunes Amours)* by
Jeremy Leah may be a first; it is certainly the first to be
openly published since the book appeared in France in
1908 under the pseudonym of 'Pierrot' (most likely that
of a Docteur Brennus).

On the surface, it is a typical 'bon bourgeois' erotic
novel of the period; there are plenty of lip-smacking,
thigh-slapping stereotypes in a plot which is more or less
engineered to suit the many and varied sexual
cavortings of its young protagonists. It offers an amusing
contrast to Alain-Fournier's lyrical *Le Grand Meaulnes*,
written five years later on the eve of the First World
War: both novels evoke a spirit of youthful innocence
and the pangs of first love in a romantic setting. There,
perhaps, the similarity ends.

THE ARTIST

Sylvie Jones studied at Camberwell School of Arts &
Crafts, London, gaining a BA in Fine Art. Well-
travelled (one of her many passions), she has held five
one-artist exhibitions and taken part in several group
shows. Her work is in many private collections and her
subject matter ranges from nudes in exotic landscapes
to illustrating the antiques page of *House & Garden*. She
divides her time between preparing for her exhibitions,
her illustrative work and an increasingly large number
of individual erotic art commissions. She lives and
works in London.

A DECLARATION OF LOVE

It was springtime. The Château de Messange, a couple of leagues from Tours, is one of the most desirable residences to be found anywhere on that enchanting level expanse which is a veritable garden of France. Its verdant terraces descend in easy stages to the side of the Loire, where the gentle murmur of the pebbly riverbed may be heard, joining together the furthest extremities of the park's generous avenues like a ribbon of silver.

The decision had been taken at the château the previous evening to go shrimping at the first light of day. Mlle Claire de Messange and her sister Marguerite, chaperoned by their highly respectable governess, Miss Ellen Anderson, would call on the way at the Château d'Estange for their close friends Jeanne and Cécile. Claude Larcher would go on ahead to spy out the spots on the river bank where their efforts were most likely to be rewarded. Finally, at the stroke of noon, all those participating in the expedition would return to Messange for lunch.

Faithful to this programme, Claude had risen early, while the stars were still in the sky, and made his way quietly down through the wooded banks to the Loire with his shrimping nets under his arm and his hands in his pockets. The affable expression on his face no doubt reflected the extremely pleasant thoughts which were running through his mind. How happy he was! He was happy because he was twenty; he was happy because of the charming existence he led at the château where every care and responsibility had been abolished; but most of all he was happy because he knew that in a moment he would be seeing again the beautiful young girl to whom he had pledged his affection, an affection which, without his realising it, bordered closely on love.

Hardly had he attained the stony stream, the goal of his expedition, before a peal of laughter announced the arrival of the girls. The latter wasted no time in setting to work, all four of them throwing themselves wholeheartedly into this new sport, each harbouring the secret ambition of filling her basket and being proclaimed the queen of the shrimping-nets.

As for Claude, the trapping of innocent creatures was barely capable of exciting in him more than cursory interest. The same thoughts that had preoccupied him earlier, as he had made his way there, filled his head as he slowly wandered upstream, absently dragging his shrimping-net through the water, to a place which was completely enclosed by foliage. He was lazily stretched out on the grass, staring into the rippling water, when a ravishing apparition suddenly appeared before him on the other side of the stream; an apparition which plunged his entire being into a state of utter confusion.

A young girl was standing there, no more than two paces from him. She was stooped over the water, as if regarding her own reflection, the very personification of every grace of youth combined with all the charms of womanhood.

Mlle Claire de Messange was eighteen years old. Her opulent blonde hair, which possessed a warmth and vibrancy all of its own, was flooded with sunlight at that particular moment as it tumbled over her shoulders, shoulders which had become exposed as a result of her madcap exertions, like a golden billow. They framed her pretty face with its high forehead, the straight line of the nose which hardly deflected the angle of her profile, her quivering nostrils and delicate ears, and ripe lips, the colour of rubies, on which a charming smile was impressed. But the most fascinating feature of this adorable face of the young girl was undoubtedly her eyes. These were blue and possessed a soft, velvety quality which seemed to fill the entire pupil completely, making her gaze seem both tender and above all mysterious at the same time.

But her entire person was quite exquisite. She was marvellously well-proportioned, slender but with the most feminine of curves. The swell of her breasts suggested all the firmness of youth; her legs and hips, which sprang out from under her close-fitting skirt, no longer recalled the shy lines of the adolescent, for all the temptations of womanhood already resided in those hips; and her neck, which was as white as satin, had a charming allure to it, an allure only associated with nascent shoulders of the most virginal variety.

Claire had left her friends for a few moments in order to refresh herself by the side of the stream. Her cheeks were slightly flushed and her pretty red lips were damp. Her eyes were shining and her bosom was heaving.

Believing herself unobserved in this remote spot, she had opened the top of her bodice in order that the breeze might cool her, and Claude, who had never seen any more of her than her face and hands, was able to admire a considerable portion of the girl's delightful young breasts. These were as white as milk and so transparent that it was easy to distinguish the tiny blue veins which ran just beneath the surface. One of them, which had almost become unseated from its cup due to all the running around and chasing which had been going on, peeped out proudly from the top of the lacework of Claire's blouse, its gorgeous crimson tip clearly visible. Her bare feet were dangling in the water, which was quite shallow at this point; her hands held up her dress and petticoats, revealing her naked legs with their dimpled calves and the bottom of her little white knickers which reached down as far as her knees, so covering them with fine lace and the most delicate needlework.

Claude, hiding in the heather no more than two steps away from the young girl, was in an almost indescribable state of excitement. With bated breath, for he was terrified of being discovered, he devoured with his eyes all the charms of his friend, charms he had never imagined to exist; this virginal apparition had propelled him into a state of ecstasy.

Suddenly the strident voice of Miss Anderson could be heard: 'Claire! Claire! Where are you? It is time for us to be making our way back to the château.'

At this sound the young girl removed her feet from the

stream, wiped them on the grass which grew to the edge of the water, and started to put on her shoes again.

First, she took out a handkerchief which she used to dry her feet, the tiny pink toenails, and her legs, where the tiny drops of water reflected the sunlight like minuscule pearls, before putting on her black stockings, which were held in place just above the knee by black garters with buckles, then she buttoned up her boots.

This last operation was the most difficult. Not having the special hook with which to do this, she had to use her bare fingers. Balanced in a semi-crouching position, leaning forward and with one foot beneath her, she tried to make do with a hairpin; as her petticoats were pulled up above her knee and her legs were apart, her most intimate lower regions were plainly exposed.

Claude, red with desire, and hardly able to keep his breath in, devoured this scene with his eyes. The girl's body was protected by her knickers, but this last veil to her modesty was made of such thin material that the pink colour of her flesh could clearly be seen through them; not only this, but the strip of material was so narrow in this place, and so stretched by the position Claire had assumed, that it moulded the part of her body it was intended to conceal in every detail.

Claude stared avidly at her delicate knees, the almost perfect contours of her thighs, well-formed at the point of their reunion with her powerful loins. Then his blood froze in his veins. Claire had modified her position so that the slit in her knickers, which had until that moment remained closed, was now wide open, clearly displaying her sexual organs, such that the young man was able to contemplate at his leisure the young girl's greatest charm, the adorable pink lips, which were of an absolutely exquisite design, shadowed from above by a light down of curly blonde hair which covered her lower abdomen and disappeared between her legs. As a consequence of the position that Claire had assumed, these lips were slightly open and revealed towards the top an exquisitely formed little bulge of pink flesh – the tiny organ of love's pleasure – like a jewel mounted in a casket.

But Claire soon got to her feet and, after having coiled her opulent blonde hair which billowed down over her shoulders, all the while looking at her reflection in the clear stream, at which she seemed to smile, charmed no doubt by the graceful image which met her eyes, she disappeared at a run in the direction from which the voice of Miss Anderson had come. The happy band immediately started back on the route to the château. Already, she was some way off, for one could no longer hear the tinkling sound of the young girls' laughter. Claude remained rooted to the spot, dreamily, feverishly even, staring at the place where the young girl had crouched, trying to prolong in his imagination the arousing vision which had only a few moments earlier been a reality.

He had been subject to an amazing revelation: that of his love for Claire de Messange. He had shared the young girl's life for more than ten years, been part of her games and her schoolwork, sat at mealtimes by her side, slept the night in an adjoining room, each considering the other like brother and sister, without it ever entering his head that in this young companion of his childhood might be found a woman; he had never touched the body of the chaste young girl in any way capable of being misconstrued, and never had his imagination conjured up before him any image which might have caused him to blush. Claude Larcher was by no means a naïve young man. Far from it, as the girls in the village could bear witness! But there is a natural carelessness about someone whom love has never prevented from falling asleep and who has no need to look for something which he finds easily among the vineyards and barns of the village where the handsome, hot-blooded women of the Tours region are loath to decline the advances of a young chap with a strapping body and a comely face.

However, in accordance with the sovereign and fatal law of affinities between people, Claude, unbeknown to himself, had been subject for a long time to the tremendous charm which the young girl emanated. He loved her without knowing it, and sometimes, as had happened that very morning, he felt wonderfully happy, experienced a sense of well-being and love which he would have been unable to explain, and which was nothing less than the instinctive response of his entire being to a question which his mind had not yet managed to formulate.

Claire also loved the young man, but in a more refined manner, as women do who have a science of the heart all of their own; she had long been aware of how powerful was the feeling which attracted her to her childhood friend. She also realised that the social differences between them, as much as that of personal wealth, ruled out any idea of marriage. But she was in no way alarmed by the tender sentiment towards him which she allowed her heart, in all its innocence, to harbour for him.

The unsettling vision of the morning, which was bound to exercise a profound influence over the lives of these two young people, had not lit an entirely unexpected fire in Claude's heart; it had only made one burn all the more brightly which had been smouldering for some little time.

Claude made not the slightest attempt to resist it. He did not even consider whether it was wrong for him to try to seduce the daughter of the man who had raised him like his own son. Like the wind during a tempest which sweeps all before it, the madness of passion, the intoxication of the flesh, had passed through him, and he felt himself vanquished. He must have Claire at any price. He would have no rest until he had slaked this frenzy of desire which drew him on just as the yawning chasm attracts a man standing on a precipice. But the lucidity of his over-stimulated mind made him understand that he would fail dismally, and that there would be no second chance, if he sought to rush the seduction of his friend. He realised that he must act slowly, a little at a time; and the boldness of his desire did not allow him to doubt for a moment that by advancing from the smallest familiarity to more delicate intimacies, from the slightest venial concession to more audacious ones, he would not manage to possess her in the manner he so wished.

From that moment his plan was laid, and he wished to put it into execution without delay. He nimbly made his way back in the direction of the château, cutting through the wood to reach the postern-gate by which the returning caravan would have to pass, where he waited impatiently, hidden amid the greenery.

A murmur of voices soon announced the return of the lady shrimpers.

Claude held his breath and his spirit was imbued with a sweet serenity when he saw that Claire was the last of the group, walking along nonchalantly, though with a certain hesitation in her step, occasionally glancing over her shoulder as if she were looking for someone; and Claude's soul was transported with delight, because he felt that it was he himself that she was looking for without perhaps being aware of the fact herself. At that moment, she stooped to pick a flower, thus allowing the group in front of her to go even further ahead. Claude rejoined her.

'My little Claire,' he said, 'you appear very thoughtful today. Is there something troubling you?'

The young girl looked up and blushed as if he were able to read her thoughts and, without answering the question, she said to him in a slightly begrudging tone:

'Why have you been avoiding me all morning? I am quite vexed with you!'

And he replied slowly, gently taking her hands in his:

'Because I only feel that I am really with you when we are alone. When you are surrounded by other people, it is as if they are always stealing a bit of you from me; it is as if the sound of your voice, the smell of your hair, all the living charms which surround you, are dispersed, profaned even, so much so that I prefer to admire you in silence from a distance rather than be contaminated by all those fortunate people who, unlike me, have no idea of their own happiness. Don't you see, Claire: I love you!'

She blushed slightly with embarrassment, her breast rising with pleasure. So Claude loved her, too! It was such a long time that she had been in love with him! She said not a word, but the radiant look of happiness which she directed at her friend was more eloquent than all the words in the world. And as she listened to him without growing angry at whatever he said, Claude raised to his mouth the hand of the young girl, which trembled slightly against his lips, but which she did not attempt to withdraw.

And he said all manner of things to her which she listened to in amazement. How charming she was thus, her mouth slightly agape as if to admit something which she did not dare to say, her pretty face red with happiness, her eyes lowered so as not to be betrayed by the light which shone in them, glowing from her morning walk.

'I love you, Claire,' he said.

And, without realising it, he had gathered her in his

arms, was pressing her against his chest, and was about to kiss her when she extricated herself. Not quickly enough to avoid the kiss being accepted and returned.

'The bell,' she said. 'They will be waiting for me at the château.'

'Will I be able to see you alone today?'

'Quite impossible.'

'This evening?'

'You're mad!'

'Perhaps, Claire, but I beg you that you must let me see you this evening. How beautiful the night is when one is in love! Let us meet here, if that suits you, and we can look at the stars together through the gaps in the foliage above our heads, and you will be more beautiful still in the soft half-light.'

'Adieu,' she repeated, before disappearing at a run. And he felt within him a joy which was beyond his control, for she had not said no.

A moment later he followed her into the dining-room at the château where lunch was served.

FIRST RENDEZVOUS

With its towers rising proudly from the steeply sloping roof, and its two wings in the style of the Renaissance enclosing the main courtyard with its flower-beds and terraces fenced in with stone balustrades, Messange, dominating as it did the surrounding plain, was a truly seigniorial residence. The Marquis André, the current proprietor of the château built by Cardinal Amboise, led a simple and extremely retired existence. Entirely devoted to the sciences, and only concerned with expanding his considerable collections in the field of natural history, he had taken little interest in the education of his two daughters, Claire and Marguerite, leaving the matter entirely in the hands of the Marquise who had, in fact, acquitted herself with some distinction in this regard.

Claude Larcher had been adopted into the life of the château on an equal footing with the others. He was the son of a childhood friend of the Marquis who had had to seek refuge in Africa, where his meagre fortune would allow him to eke out an existence of sorts, after ruining himself in business; he had not wished to be encumbered by a son in such a perilous expedition so far from home. The owner of the château and his wife, who had hoped at one time for a male heir of their own, had found Claude a most agreeable guest, not only because of his honesty and gaiety but, above all, because of his charming childlike figure and eyes sparkling with intelligence. The Marquis was particularly attached to him, and instructed him in Latin and the sciences, but the handsome little chap preferred to play the giddy goat out in the fields rather than ponder over his schoolbooks. If we briefly mention in passing little Marguerite, Claire's sister, and Germaine, their chambermaid, we will have met all the main characters we shall encounter in this story.

It would be superfluous to say that Claude awaited impatiently the time of the rendezvous given to him that morning by his friend. As soon as night fell, and his hosts had retired to their private apartments, he furtively let himself out of the château and made his way to the side of the pond where we accompanied him this morning with Claire, next to a bench almost entirely covered by the canopy of a magnificent willow tree. He sat down on this bench, which he had not mentioned to the young girl, though he knew she would come to find him there, for there is a book in which all these things are written that only lovers know how to read. His mind, still greatly stimulated by the arousing sight he had witnessed earlier, gave a particular shape to his dreams of love. Claire was already by his side, he was speaking to her, he could smell her, he was covering her with kisses. His wait did not cause him the least concern; had he not seen Claire's love for him shine from her eyes? His heart told him that she would come, and the heart is never mistaken.

And, in fact, at that moment she appeared at the

intersection of two of the paths, craning her neck and looking absolutely charming in the pale, clear moonlight.

In less than a moment, Claude was by her side. He guided her gently into the shadows and, sitting her on a mound of grass, he kneeled at her feet. She did not even dream of opposing this silent advance, obedient and as if impassive in the face of this great torrent of passion, the thrill of which communicated itself even to her. Delicately inclining her head towards him, as if to reassure him of her feelings with regard to him, she let him stroke her trembling fingers and legs, while his kisses slowly climbed up her black stockings as far as the knee, down to which her knickers almost reached.

Then she pulled him towards her. He pressed his lips against those of Claire, who did not turn her head away, while he squeezed her in his arms and against his chest.

They remained like this for some time, mouth to mouth, their two bodies tightly interlaced. Claude drank in the young girl's breath, became intoxicated with the odour of her fresh skin and the perfume of her fine hair, was beside himself with joy at holding in his arms the ravishing apparition of the morning. Heart to heart, he could feel the quickening of her pulse; the pair of them were breathless with the same delicious fear, a fear in which their two beings became united. Claire had closed her eyes, the emotion of the scene turning her white at the moment of their embrace. They exchanged only stray words, kisses replacing the sound of language. They were overwhelmed with a

tremendous sense of happiness which made tears of
ecstasy rise in their throats and tears of joy form in their
eyes.

Little by little, he tilted her backwards against the
thick moss growing on the bank of the moat behind
them, just as one might place a baby in its cot, while the
object of his affections held his head next to hers with
her arms.

Claire was now looking at him with an undisguised
expression of love in her eyes, and Claude immediately
wanted to cover her pretty face with kisses. Knowing
the entire scale of loving embraces, he gently pressed his
lips against her eyes, her temples, the top of her
forehead just where the hair starts to grow, then his lips
moved down to caress her ears, which he tickled until
she laughed, and then, moving lower still, he reached
her neck, which he kissed ardently before eventually
burying his lips in the back of her neck.

While he held her there trembling under his burning
kisses, Claude had almost imperceptibly allowed his
hand to stray from round her waist until he could gently
squeeze her breasts, which he felt stiffen under her
dress. A mad urge took hold of him to caress them as
well. He had already furtively unbuttoned the top of
Claire's dress when, suddenly growing afraid, she
stopped him with her hand.

'Darling Claude,' she said, 'you must spare my blushes:
what you are doing is wrong and it hurts me.'

But Claude, passing his left hand under the young
girl's head, stooped down and covered her charming

little mouth with ardent kisses; he even gently slipped his tongue, which sought out and found hers, between her lips. At that moment the whole of Claire's body seemed to become limp. In the grip of such an overwhelming sensation, she was on the point of fainting. Thinking the moment propitious, Claude quickly undid the rest of the buttons on her dress and energetically unlaced the top of her corset, which he pulled apart, breaking the ribbon which held together the neck of her chemise as he did so.

When Claire, recovering herself with a hollow sigh, tried to struggle free, the young man had already liberated her splendid breasts, whose crimson nipples were quite erect, and thrown himself like some ravenous beast on this palpitating, virginal flesh which he fondled and kissed frenetically, burying his nose and mouth between her breasts as if to lose himself there. While the young girl still struggled to push him away, he swallowed a mouthful of the perfumed flesh of her bubs, with their skin as soft as that of peaches, as if he wanted to eat them, rubbing the entire length of his tongue over them while vigorously rolling her nipples between his fingers, which he then began to suck just a child sucks at its mother's breast. Claire, overwhelmed by the pleasure of being touched for the first time in her life like this, no longer had the strength to mount any resistance; she yielded to him despite herself, while a sob rose in her throat.

By this time, they were close together again. It is said that the silvery words of lovers, promising always to be true to one another, is like a celestial music. Claude by now had one hand negligently draped over his lover's body; pressing down, almost by chance, he clearly felt beneath the thin material of her dress the lower part of her stomach, where the legs join together. All the blood immediately drained from his heart. He remembered the decision he had reached that very morning not to run any risk which might lead to him losing her. But what he had just been allowed to experience had caused the greatest confusion imaginable in all his senses; he felt as if he was going mad, and the sight he had been vouchsafed that morning of all her most intimate charms was too much for him.

He distracted Claire with kisses, lifting up the hem of her dress as he did so and gently sliding his hand between her legs. His hand touched her knees, he could feel the bottom of her knickers, and still he groped upwards between her thighs, seeking an opening in the garments which clothed her most intimate places. Then, like a madman, he cast all prudence to the wind and with a sudden movement grabbed her about the loins, holding the sweet girl's sexual parts in the palm of his hand. He could feel the rub of her little blonde pubis against his wrist. The two little love lips made an incredibly gentle impression on his hand; he could feel their dampness. He eased his finger into the opening and found a little hillock which was quite hard. He was just about to stroke it when Claire, coming to her senses at last, violently pushed Claude's hand away and managed to break away from his embrace.

In a voice in which there was as much sadness as irritation she said to him:

'Never try to do that again, Claude, or we shall not be friends. Love me like I love you; but I must have your respect.'

Claire, in fact, was of an unsullied purity. Brought up under her mother's eyes, she knew nothing whatsoever about love, or even about the pleasure of the senses. Imbued with an extreme sense of natural prudishness, she considered it a terrible blow to her self-respect that Claude had thought it permissible to place his hand on the secret parts of her body, parts which she herself had not even begun to explore.

Brought suddenly down to earth in this way, Claude was utterly crestfallen, and extremely vexed with himself, since he realised that in trying to go too fast, he could well have compromised his entire plan of seduction. He reproached himself for his lack of control over his own senses, and he stammered out an apology.

Faced with such genuine despair, Claire felt her anger evaporate, and she forgave him in the kindest way, and the pair of them, with their arms wrapped round each other's waists, slowly made their way back to the château.

THE STORY OF A LASCIVIOUS
CHAMBERMAID

We have already mentioned that Mlle Germaine was the young girls' chambermaid. Her description: physically rather pretty, with thick hair, dark, unfathomable eyes, thin at the waist yet endowed with an ample cleavage; blithely gainsaying her twenty-five springs. All in all, with the exception of her dress, a perfect example of those crafty soubrettes which it is such a delight to ogle at the theatre through a pair of opera-glasses.

Morally speaking: an intelligent Parisian lass without the slightest scruple. Having only arrived at Messange ten months earlier, she had not managed to claim any great intimacy with the proud young girl who, as we have seen, was little disposed to encourage the familiarities of a chambermaid, even if the same was not true of little Marguerite.

The story of her life, which is pretty much the story of the Parisian underworld, is nonetheless original and merits closer attention.

Born of impoverished parents, she had spent her childhood in the streets with children the same age as herself, playing games, running wild, and commandeering as her own the ruined fortifications near where she lived, as abandoned as the weeds which grow in the cracks between the paving stones in such run-down districts. Is there anything more precocious that the children of the poor you find in Paris? Just examine such old fortifications, and you will see boys and girls playing together with the most remarkable freedom.

Young Germaine had also experienced this same life of precocious pleasures. At first, she had valiantly avoided such sexual intimacy, which she found frightening, but that had set the nerves of the other boys and girls on edge. The brunette was pretty and well-proportioned, everyone fancied her, and her natural reserve annoyed her comrades. A lad who was looked up to by the rest, because he was the strongest of the bunch, had tried to overcome her resistance, that is to say that he had made her lie on the grass and tried to lift up her skirt. But the young girl had defended herself so vigorously and shouted so loudly that the urchin had been forced to take to his heels, his curiosity unsatisfied. She had made friends with a fair-haired girl her age, who had been allowed to kiss and stroke her face. Sometimes she had even rapidly passed her hand between Germaine's legs, touching her private parts, which she longed to stroke, through the slit in her drawers. Sometimes, too, half-sitting in front of her, unfastening her own skirt and holding apart her knickers with her left hand while with the other she stroked her little hole, this friend would insert her finger in the middle and vigorously move it in and out over the little pink hillock towards the top of her sex while begging Germaine to render this service for her. While she did this, her face would become red, her breathing faster, her eyes would shine with pleasure, and her body twitch nervously at the moment of orgasm, after which she would lie back in a faint, clearly proving that the demonstration was nothing if not sincere.

Young Germaine, excited by such lascivious spectacles, would have liked deep down to experience such unknown pleasures for herself, but she was much too shy to try.

In the end, some kids, resentful and not a little inflamed by this resistance which they had never encountered before, plotted together to obtain by force that which had been refused to them until that moment. This was October time, and night had fallen more quickly than usual due to the dark clouds which filled the sky. With the pretext of playing a game, the young girl had been conducted to a deserted corner of the neighbourhood. One of the boys, who had agreed to act as look-out, gave the pre-arranged signal.

At that moment the others collectively took hold of Germaine and upended her on the grass. The girl, sensible as she was, put up a valiant fight, biting one, kicking another, begging the boys to leave her alone; but numbers were against her, and she was soon overpowered. Stretched out on her back, two of them secured her arms while two more held her feet; then, with eyes sparkling with curiosity, the boys lifted up her dress and underskirts as far as the waist; but as her pair of little white knickers prevented everyone from being able to see what they wanted to see, one of the girls who had been in the plot with the boys stepped forward, unbuttoned them and pulled them off over her boots. While keeping her skirt hitched up over her waist, her legs were forced wide apart, and everyone present, boys and girls alike, was able to satisfy their lubricious curiosity with regard to the girl's ravishing body, with its clearly delineated stomach and hips, with its thighs, firm and dimpled, separated at the junction with the lower abdomen by a charming delicate cleft like the two lips of a bright red mouth, and covered in soft light brown hair. But even this sight did not suffice for them: they turned her over in order to admire her beautiful little bottom, with its firm, well-rounded buttocks, the skin soft and white; then one of the boys parted her buttocks slightly, to the great joy of all present, and revealed her tiny crinkled rose lost at the bottom of a narrow valley. She was turned back over again, and everyone awaited their turn to caress her pink little slit and rub the crimson button, which seemed rather large for her age. Then Germaine's blonde friend, who had being dying to do this for ages, pressed through the throng of boys and, amidst their enthusiastic and ribald cries, knelt between the girl's thighs and began to lick her sexual parts avidly. Pushing back with her finger the pretty red lips, her tongue moved back and forth along the entire length of the slit, then she rolled the clitoris between her lips and flicked it rapidly with the tip of her tongue. After this game had been going on for a certain time, Germaine's stomach began to heave up and down and her thighs were racked with a nervous spasm. The crowd drew closer, fascinated by what was happening. 'She's coming! She's coming! Go on, Thérèse! You can't stop now, she's about to come!' Thérèse did not need telling twice where her duty lay.

While this was going on, two boys, visibly excited, had been enjoying themselves lifting up Thérèse's skirts, who pretended not to notice; and while one of them, coiling his hand round the back of her thighs, had managed to insert one finger in the little hole between the buttocks and another into her vagina (Thérèse had lost her virginity in this way long ago) which he then rubbed briskly, the other lad, with his hand across her lower abdomen, gave her a good wanking; this time, it was Thérèse's turn to squeeze her thighs convulsively as she began to climax.

Indeed, as the lads had remarked, and in spite of the anger that this unexpected attack had caused in her, Germaine, who was by temperament a sensual brunette, though such feelings had been repressed in her until now, really did seem to have been overwhelmed by this new pleasure and was on the point of orgasm. Her face became very red and her breath became short and spasmodic; a muffled sound came from her throat, she arched her hips faster and faster, and her thighs gripped the blonde head of Thérèse as if she wanted to suffocate her. But Thérèse, who knew all the signs, recognised the onset of the final spasm, and forgot all about her own pleasure as she licked the young girl with increasing ardour, paying attention now only to her clitoris. All the teenagers, boys and girls alike, all extremely excited, now crept closer in order to watch the orgasm of their victim. Germaine, reaching the final spasm, suddenly stretched out her back as a long exclamation of pleasure came from her throat, and her fists clenched and unclenched uncontrollably; and a small jet of warm liquid squirted from the narrow slit and splashed Thérèse in the face before she had time to move it away. She herself was reaching her final voluptuous spasm and rolled heavily onto the grass.

Everybody present shouted 'Bravo!', delighted with the success of their scheme; and, excited beyond control by this enticing display, they fell one upon the other in lascivious embrace, which was their usual pastime. They demonstrated their kindness to the poor girl who, ridden with shame, was hiding her face in her hands. They helped her to her feet, consoled her as best they could concerning her misadventure, and promised that they would never play such a trick on her again. Cunning young rogues that they were, they knew that Germaine's encounter with pleasure had won her over to their cause. Which, in fact, was exactly what happened. She accepted Thérèse's kisses and caresses, returned them in her turn, had all sorts of other young friends and, like them, also accommodated herself to the lubricious pleasures of boys. The latter wasted no time in deflowering her, despite her youthfulness, their fingers helping them out should their masculinity prove unequal to the task.

Later, Germaine got a job folding paper at the commercial printer's on the Rue de Rome and, like her companions, became the mistress of a typesetter.

Her lover, a tremendous expert in all the games of love, completed her education in this subject. She learned all there was to know, for he liked everything there was to like, this being the way of his natural inclinations. She found an equal pleasure in offering to her lover the marvellous grotto of love encased in its thick fleece of soft curly hair or her tiny rosette hidden in the cleft between two buttocks of an awesome beauty. Her adorable mouth, with its sensual lips, became experienced at kissing his entire body, but especially the sword of love, and procuring for him every nuance of voluptuousness. Her flexible hips lent themselves admirably to all the acrobatics of sexual passion; yet, even so, there were times when she missed the intimate caresses of girls her own age. Her lover, despite all his expertise, could not rival the infinite delicacy of her female friends whose soft caresses procured for her the supreme delights of orgasm and plunged her into an ecstasy of enchantment.

One day, as she was delivering some packets of visiting-cards to an elegant doxy on the Boulevard Haussmann (Germaine was twenty by this time), the latter found her so beguiling with her dark eyes, which set off her face admirably, that she immediately enrolled her into her service on wages that Germaine could not refuse.

Of all the schooling in sexual pleasure she had been through until that day, nothing could compare with what she learned in this fashionable house of easy

morals. The day after she had entered into the service
of Mme Blanche d'Antigny, her mistress rang for her. As
it was not yet midday, she was still in bed. She signalled
Germaine to approach.

'Come closer, my child,' she said, taking her hands,
'and let us talk together. How do you like being in my
service?'

'Oh, very much, Madame. It is very beautiful here
and you have been so kind to me.'

'You realise that being in my service means that
sometimes you will have things to do which are – which
are, well, rather delicate? Do you understand me? There
are gentlemen, and ladies, who come to see me; if they
find you pretty, it is very important that you do not
displease them by being coy with them. If, from time to
time, they want to kiss you, or caress you a bit, you will
let them do so, it's not the end of the world. Tell me,
little one, could you get used to that sort of life?'

Germaine, pretending not to understand, lowered her
eyes without replying.

'Well, at least you don't say no. I think that we shall
get on famously together. What I ask of you has nothing
disagreeable about it, especially when one is as pretty
and well-formed as you are. What's more, your
complaisance in these matters will earn you all manner
of little presents, which friends like to give to each
other. Do you really think you could get used to it, tell
me?'

'But Madame… If it's absolutely necessary… I will do
my best to please you… I don't refuse…'

'That's right! Very well said! You're so nice I could eat you! In fact, come here and give me a sign of your eagerness to please me. Kiss me.'

While Germaine obeyed her mistress, the latter, holding her with one arm, undid the buttons on her blouse with the other, so displaying her breasts.

'What youthfulness! How firm they are! But this is just the start. What I see here makes me curious to see the rest.'

Germaine felt the hand of her mistress straying beneath her petticoats.

'Please, Madame, not that,' she said, for the sake of appearances.

'What a body! Your skin is like satin! I would give a year of my life to spend a night with you as your lover. And those curly pubes of yours!'

'But, please, Madame, I don't have a lover.'

'No lover! With a face as beautiful as yours, it's not possible! One should not hoard such things for one's own benefit. You are making a great mistake. If you don't like men, perhaps you like little girls of your own age, which is not so bad either.'

Mme Blanche embraced Germaine again and began to play with her more intimate charms in a more determined manner than she had done until then.

'Wasn't I right when I said that you prefer the tender caresses of little girls like yourself to those of clumsy great men?'

'As you say, Madame, they are certainly more agreeable,' said Germaine, who saw the direction in which her mistress was headed.

'Here's to happiness! I am sure that we will soon be great friends, unless I seem too old to you, or you find me repugnant.'

'But, on the contrary, Madame is very pretty.'

'A little flattery never hurt! But I wouldn't be so pretty if I didn't have full recourse to all the artifices of my toilette, whereas you, you are pretty without anything, and that is the sign of true beauty.'

Even as she said this, the caresses of Germaine's mistress became more intimate.

'Please, Madame... I don't know what to say... I'm very excited...'

Mme Blanche increased her caresses, concentrating now entirely on the clitoris, which she masturbated enthusiastically.

'What big eyes you have, you little rogue. You are about to come!'

Germaine allowed herself to fall on the bed:

'Yes, Madame... Yes, Madame... I am coming... Oh, I'm com... com... com... Oh...!'

Mme Blanche, extremely excited herself as a result of this little game, jumped nimbly onto the foot of the bed, arranging Germaine, who was so enchanted by the direction events had taken that she allowed herself to be used in this way with complete docility, in the position that suited her; then, throwing back her skirt and petticoats over her face, Mme Blanche placed her head between the delightful thighs of her pretty maid, attaching her mouth greedily to the places that her hand had a few moments before been rubbing, and began to lick, suck and bite them until Germaine gave sign that she had managed a second time to savour the supreme spasm of voluptuousness.

When the young girl had recovered from this experience, Mme Blanche asked her gently if she would care to return the same favour. Without waiting for a reply, she quickly stripped off her chemise, presenting her splendid nakedness to the enchanted eyes of her maid, lay down upon the bed, kissed Germaine, and suggested seductively in her ear that she might like to undress as well. In a trice, she too appeared in all the radiant beauty of her nakedness before her mistress, whose eyes sparkled as she enumerated without hesitation all her charms, making the beautiful girl turn around before her, as she looked on in ecstatic rapture, so that she could admire her from every angle. Then, beckoning her to the bed, she covered her in kisses and, fired with the same desire to reach orgasm in the embrace of this ravishing child, she made her kneel before her, took her head in her hands, and guided it between her thighs, to that very same place which had given Germaine so much pleasure a moment earlier. Germaine did not resist, excited and delighted in her turn at being able to rub her little muzzle in the white, sweetly perfumed flesh of her beautiful mistress. Her hands parted the thick blonde pubic mat of her mistress, and her tongue quickly found the thick button of love lodged between her lips, like a ruby in a casket of crimson velvet. Consummate as she was in such matters, she soon made her lubricious mistress, who was delighted to discover that she had taken on such a talented protégée, writhe and moan with pleasure under her exquisite caresses.

It is unnecessary to mention that this pretty duet engaged in the same activities several times more that same afternoon, and that the elegant courtesan was absolutely enchanted by her pretty, not to say extremely obliging, little maid. Nor is it necessary to enter into the details of the numerous piquant adventures that befell Germaine's lot in this highly civilised house of love. A number of friends of the house partook of this succulent dish, as they thought of her, which was truly fit for a king.

So how, you might be wondering, did someone with such a liberal education in the seductive arts manage to enter into the service of the Marquise de Messange?

Mme Blanche's lovers preferred the pretty young maid to her mistress. The latter finally took umbrage and was no longer willing to allow her maid to make up a threesome in her pleasures. Germaine, for her part, decided to give in her notice; in any event, her health was unequal to the exhausting life she was leading in Paris. She retired to her aunt's house in Touraine and sought a position, with the intention of so regaining her strength as a result of light duties in elegant surroundings, in one of the numerous châteaux which are to be found in this highly attractive part of the world. Germaine's aunt, Mme Marneffe, who was as well known at Messange as her services were appreciated, suggested her niece to the Marquise. The latter, impressed by the girl's intelligence and transparent honesty, immediately took her into her service without making further enquiry.

We shall encounter her again in the course of this story.

LOVE'S SKIRMISHES

Claire and Claude, our gentle lovers, continued to love each other, one with all the poetry of her virgin soul, the other with all the ardour of his twenty birthdays; and this love increased in the same proportion as they became more familiar with each other and their two souls learned to understand one another.

The adorable young girl utterly abandoned herself to this sentiment, the supreme pleasure of natures such as hers which are sweet and affectionate. Just as the butterfly fascinated by the flame will singe its iridescent wings of every colour of the rainbow, so do children yield themselves to a love whose radiant voluptuousness is all they know. Is not the whole of life summarised in the single word: 'Love'?

In the course of those delightful summer evenings whose unsettling poetry it is impossible to describe, in the park at Messange full of the smells of the forest, at the very same place, beside the pond with its white water-lilies and its reeds impregnated with the light of the moon, where they had exchanged their first vows, Claire and her friend often returned to find that solitude which is so dear to lovers. Eventually, such was their need for each other that hardly a day would go by without our two young lovers making their way there to embrace each other tightly in one of those protracted kisses in which one places one's entire soul.

And each time they met was more enchanting than the previous time, their kisses ever more delicious, their caresses more agreeable. Their very words became the softest music which cradled their love and made it more exalted through the unspoken promise of its eternal duration.

Claire no longer had any reason to complain about those tentative sexual experiences which had once frightened her. In truth, the young man was so fearful of poisoning a love which had by now entirely conquered him and become his whole life that he seemed to have forgotten the physical aspect of his passion. The truth, however, was that the simple desire he had felt during the shrimping expedition had become an uncontrollable rage with him ever since passion had come into his soul and he had discovered more and more about the adorable charms of his loved one. The truth of the matter was that he suffered considerable distress during these meetings at which the young girl was entirely at his mercy, and he had to muster every ounce of self-control at his command in order not to scream out his desire like a rutting animal and satisfy himself there and then. And, finally, the truth was that this torture could not continue indefinitely and that soon, as he well knew, though the fact saddened him, the masculine side of him, eager for possession, would once again take control.

One day, after Claire and her parents had been picnicking with their friends at the Château d'Estange, they had been detained until late in the evening.

Despite the pleasure she took at being in the company of her friends, Claire was very saddened at having spent an entire day without having seen Claude, who had not been included in the party of young girls. Claude, for his part, was equally afflicted at not having seen his friend; from his bedroom, unwilling to go to bed until he had at least given her a kiss, he watched out for her return to the château.

He heard her come in around eleven o'clock. After thinking matters over carefully, he removed his boots, so that he would not be heard in the corridor, and dashed along the corridor in the darkness to Claire's bedroom door, which he opened and went in as it was never locked.

'Claire, are you already in bed?' he asked.

'Yes, Claude. What a surprise, your coming here!'

'It's because I haven't seen you all day long and I really want to kiss you.'

'Very well, my love, but you must go away immediately afterwards so that no one catches you here.'

'How sweet you are, my darling Claire! Let me kneel down by your bed so that even if I can't see you, I can feel your presence by my side for a moment.'

The young girl consented to what her friend asked of her. Claude leaned over her, covering her face with passionate kisses and holding her lips against his own in a long, feverish embrace. Then, unbuttoning her nightgown, he plunged his face into the expanse of virginal and fragrant flesh, licking the erect tips of her nipples, fondling them in the cup of his hand. The familiar perfume of his beloved's long blonde hair, mingled with the delicate odour of her armpits, filled him with desire and brought to his mind more intimate memories still until he was truly drunk with passion.

An irresistible desire seized hold of him to know all the secrets of this delicious body, those hidden parts which are the very essence of woman and about which he had long been consumed with curiosity. The sex instinct secretly gnawed at him, his pulse raced until he became almost dizzy... What was more, the entire situation was so exciting, the young girl he loved, lying almost beneath him, with her breasts uncovered...

Claire, in all her youthful innocence, had been a prize well worth the capture. Suddenly, she clutched his arm, trembling like a leaf, and said:

'Quiet!'

The sound of footsteps on the stairs could be heard. It was the marquis on his way to bed. And Claude had left the door ajar behind him! Claire held her breath, waiting for her father to pass. Claude saw in a flash that the young girl was utterly without defence and could not resist him without being caught. With a wild movement, he threw back the bedclothes, hitched up her nightdress, and slipped his hand between her thighs, forcing them apart, until he touched her sexual organs.

Claire, half-distracted, made but a feeble resistance, hardly daring to move nor use any force from fear of making a noise and so drawing attention to herself. Tears streamed down her face as she tried with both hands to push her nightdress down below her waist, so

preventing Claude from taking further advantage.

Her father's step, close by, made one of the floorboards in the corridor creak; at that moment, Claire, terrified, stopped defending herself. Claude had full possession of the young girl's sexual parts which he caressed ardently, moving his finger up and down in the narrow slit and stroking the clitoris which he discovered to be large and erect. But that was not sufficient to assuage his thirst to possess this delicious body: he parted her thighs with his two hands and avidly placed his mouth against the young girl's most intimate lips. He could feel the heat of her body; the usual odour, not at all unpleasant, emanated from the tiny slit which was extremely damp. He was just about to make Claire experience the spasm of love with his tongue, when the marquis was heard turning the key in his door. With a tremendous effort, Claire tore herself free, violently pushing Claude away from her, and jumped out of bed. Then, without a single word being uttered, she took him by the arm and showed him out of the room, locking the door behind him.

For a week they were at daggers drawn. Claire did not say a word to him, pretending not to see him and, even at the table, seemed to be utterly unaware of his presence. She never went out alone, and spent the entire afternoon by her mother's side.

Claude was in a state of despair, he believed their rupture would be permanent, and since he loved her with all his heart, he moved about with his head bowed, as if weary. The Marquise asked him about the state of

his health at mealtimes, and Claire was forced to take
stock of her friend's lamentable condition. How he
loved her! How could he live without her love? He had
told her so many times in the past, but the proof was
amazing to see. Claire was moved to the very depths of
her soul. Certainly, what Claude had done was very
wicked, and in her innocence she vainly interrogated
her mind in order to understand what pleasure he could
find in such indecencies which deeply offended her
sense of modesty, at the same time as causing an
indefinable emotion in her, but her anger could not hold
out long against his love.

Among the fatal laws regulating the life of the soul,
there is one which is admitted by everyone, because
everyone has experienced it many times, and that is the
desire to see places for which we retain a happy memory.
A fragment of our soul would seem to have remained
there, and so this place where we have known our most
intense experiences is like a part of ourselves.

It was a sentiment such as this which the two children
obeyed as they prowled around the pond with the white
water-lilies, hoping to find under the willow the corner
of earth where they had fallen in love with each other.
One afternoon, as she made her way there with a heavy
heart, she saw Claude sitting in his customary spot: the
poor dear boy was crying. In a single movement she was
by his side, kneeling at his feet, and removing the
handkerchief which was covering his face. Then,
pressing her lips against his, she proved to him by means
of a long, silent kiss all her compassion and how much

she loved him, even as she felt her friend's tears trickling down her own cheeks, for Claude was still crying, only now he was crying tears of joy.

And the young girl coquettishly threw back her ravishing head, took a step backwards in order to contemplate her friend, and stared him steadily in the eye, looking at him in such a way that Claude could read in her expression an infinite tenderness and her pardon for all his wrongs. They kissed each other gently on the lips and softly exchanged some words before returning to the château, holding each other about the waist just as they used to do.

THE TITILLATING ADVENTURES OF A CHAMBERMAID

We left Germaine shortly after her arrival at the Château de Messange.

Her special duties consisted of looking after the two young girls: Claire and Marguerite. This château's Parisian inhabitant was delighted by her new circumstances. The superb country residence enchanted her, and the milieu in which she now found herself was like having her virginity all over again.

But such an ideal could not avoid falling victim to the lot of all roses. Her background, and above all her natural inquisitiveness, soon meant that she realised which side her bread was buttered on.

The first person to benefit from this was another servant at the château, a well-built young peasant, who quickly attracted the attention and the admiration of the young woman. Claude stumbled over them one day as he was strolling round the gardens. Hearing a noise coming from a barn used to store the hay, he was able to creep up without being seen and found himself confronted by a most arousing spectacle. Germaine and the coachman, whose name was Jean, were caught in the act, but there was nothing particularly refined about their activity, it was simply the coupling of the male and female in all its brutal savagery, and in all its magnificent power. Germaine, irresistibly attracted by the man's virility, so different from all the affectations you find in Paris, had followed Jean. Now she was defending her honour, much as she might desire him, not wishing to concede without the show of a struggle, like every girl does. But this was without reckoning on her mighty partner. Jean, excited beyond endurance by her resistance, took her in his arms and almost threw her in the hay without paying the least heed to her protestations. Ignoring the treasures of her ample cleavage, he hitched up her dress, petticoats and chemise above the waist, and prised open her legs in order to linger over the sight of her sex. Then, holding her in this position with one hand, he unbuttoned his trousers with the other and took out his enormous rod.

Thick and long, red from the rush of blood and furrowed by a network of blue veins, it looked as hard as an iron bar; the head of his penis, completely uncovered by his foreskin, was more like a bludgeon. At the sight of it, Germaine became afraid.

'Jean, my love. Please, no; you won't get it in. You will hurt me! Please, Jean!'

She defended herself, clenching her thighs, pushing down her dress with both hands, trying to free herself. But Jean was by far the stronger; he had soon laid out Germaine's charming body once again, plainly exposing her sexual organs for all to see, then, placing his enormous member at the entrance of the young woman's charming little quim, he took the weight of his body on his arms and began to push, moving his backside back and forth, and breathing like a rutting beast.

Germaine, realising that all resistance was useless, resigned herself, somewhat anxiously, to her lot, for only the head of his virile member had penetrated her, and the violent shafting motions of her partner made her worry whether she was about to be torn asunder. Finally, little by little, he had fully entered her. Such is the wonderful elasticity of the side of the vagina, that her dainty grotto of love swallowed this enormous charge without the least ill effect. Germaine closed her eyes; and the sound of her breath coming by fits and starts could be heard.

Claude watched the enormous member moving back and forth. At first motionless, Germaine now began to move her thighs and the entire length of her body started to tremble. Suddenly, she arched her stomach and squeezed her fists. Her vulva, which had stretched due to all the effort it had expended, gripped her lover's rod tightly, and the resulting contact of these two tremendous sexual organs had caused a revolution throughout her entire being. An extraordinary sensation, a climax such as she had never experienced before, had completely taken possession of her; it was as if she had been injected with fire in her veins. She cried aloud, so great was her pleasure.

'Yes, Jean. Yes, yes! Quicker! Like that, yes! Yes! I'm coming! I'm coming! Oh! I can feel your come inside me!'

And she gripped the body of her lover, coiling her arms about him, squeezing him between her febrile thighs which she crossed behind his back, as he squirted his bubbling semen deep into her vagina while uttering exclamation of the most utter sexual satisfaction. They remained like this, riveted one to the other, for a long while, each savouring in silence the voluptuous pleasure of the moment. Finally Jean, extracting himself from the passionate embrace of his ravishing and radiant mistress, slowly withdrew his member from the body of the beautiful young woman, and the white liquid of love dribbled from her crimson vulva across her buttocks in elegant testimony of the copious nature of his ejaculation: Germaine's thighs were completely inundated.

This scene, as violent as it was unexpected, had

utterly overwhelmed Claude. His blood was boiling in his veins, an irresistible ardour had seized hold of him, even as he had watched events unfurl, and his hands had automatically clutched at his rod which had become swollen and enormous notwithstanding the fact that it was impeded by his trousers. He had unbuttoned his flies and, taking his burning erection in one hand, assisted matters in the natural manner such that, at the very same time as Germaine and her partner, he too had experienced the same spasm which had left him inundated with the same hot liquid.

For the next few days the young man could think of nothing else but what he had witnessed, he even dreamed about it. A strong urge took hold of him to possess the young woman physically himself.

He resisted the impulse however, not wishing to profane the love he harboured for Claire, realising the extent of his betrayal towards his charming friend should he become the lover of a woman employed in her service. But how can one resist a desire so intense that it follows you everywhere like a shadow without giving you a moment's peace? 'After all, love has nothing to do with it,' he said to himself, 'it's just an animal instinct that will go away again as soon as it has been satisfied!'

Unable to bear it a moment longer, one evening he made his way to Germaine's bedroom just at the moment that she was preparing for bed and was half-undressed; in fact, all she had on was her chemise, and even that had slipped from her shoulders to reveal the young woman's firm pink breasts which stood up

proudly. He remained in the doorway for a moment unable to make up his mind, seized at the same time with admiration for the girl's almost naked body and trepidation at his audacious conduct. Germaine quickly backed away from him, red with surprise; she reached for her clothes, but Claude did not give her time to put anything on. Casting aside his earlier hesitation, he closed and bolted the door behind him and threw himself on the young girl, sweeping her into his arms, and kissing her on the mouth, the neck, and on her ravishing breasts, having prised away Germaine's arms with which she sought to protect herself, while his lascivious hand lost itself between Germaine's thighs, fondling the young woman's most intimate charms beneath the thin cloth of her chemise, feeling the rustle of her pubic hair and the soft, warm sensation of her sexual parts under his fingers.

Germaine, taken by surprise by this unexpected attack, only defended herself feebly, more for the sake of form than anything else, because she was in reality overjoyed by such an adventure. She found Claude very attractive, and she had already considered trying to seduce him. Thus, even while feeling herself the prey of this handsome youth, whose ardent kisses reigned down on her mouth, her breasts became erect, her entire being quivered under his passionate caresses, and a powerful urge to possess him seized hold of her. She utterly abandoned herself to Claude who, realising she was his, guided her to the bed and lay down next to her but upside down. He raised her chemise and, fascinated by her naked body, applied his mouth to the part that his hand had just been exciting. He kissed Germaine greedily, taking her vulva in his mouth and sucking her clitoris, which was already hard, while she for her part bucked up and down under his luxurious embrace, squeezing the young man's head between her thighs.

After a moment, Claude pulled his head away, rolled over on his back, and pulled Germaine's body on top of him in such a manner that his head remained between the beautiful girl's thighs. He slipped his hands beneath her buttocks and redoubled the passionate stroking motions he was making along the entire length of her clitoris. Meanwhile the sexual odour of her vulva made him almost drunk with excitement as he forced his tongue into the warm depths of her vagina, and he breathed in the smell of the moist juices which emanated from her sexual parts, stimulated by all the rubbing they had received.

Germaine, in the grip of pleasure, was panting and writhing about uncontrollably on the bed. Her head was turned in the direction of Claude's feet; she unbuttoned his breeches and took out his gorgeous member, hot and swollen with desire. First she stroked it, then she placed it in her mouth, sucking it passionately, in this way repaying Claude for the kisses she had received. But Claude was too excited to restrain himself and would have come almost immediately had he not moderated Germaine's enthusiasm.

'Wait,' he cried, 'not so fast. That way we can both come at the same time.'

Thrusting his head once again between the thighs of the beautiful girl, he redoubled his caresses, letting his tongue wander all over her lower abdomen and buttocks, exploring every crevice and licking the little wrinkled pink hole, whose elasticity he tested by inserting his entire finger. This he did so easily that he proved that this charming place was no stranger to Cupid's virile member.

In the throes of such lascivious caresses and mutual excitement, the young couple uttered a stream of pleasurable exclamations. Claude began once again to lick the engorged clitoris of the young woman as he seized hold of her swollen breasts with their erect nipples. One could tell that Germaine was approaching the supreme pleasure from the manner in which her sexual organs began to swell, the febrile nature of her movements, the almost frantic manner in which she clasped her partner, and the energetic manner in which she masturbated Claude while taking his entire rod in her mouth.

Suddenly she let out a gasp and entirely stopped what she was doing. At the same time Claude felt his face grow wet. Rather than withdrawing though, he squeezed the fragrant vulva between his lips and swallowed the milky fluid which was squirting out. He himself had arrived at the pinnacle of pleasure and, feeling his lover's sexual spasm, he lost control of himself and filled his lover's mouth with his burning sperm. Germaine, who loved the white liquid of love, was careful not to open her lips; squeezing his rod with her hand to choke off the release of the sperm, she allowed it to escape only a little at a time, so prolonging her friend's pleasure, swallowing it drop by drop, so as not to waste the least particle.

It would be superfluous to remark how delighted our two lovers were by their adventure and the intoxicating nature of the voluptuous sensations they experienced in each other's arms. Germaine, elated at possessing a lover who was so gentle with her, covered him in kisses and the tenderest caresses. She undressed Claude so that he was quite naked and she could study his splendid, svelte body. For his part, Claude removed Germaine's chemise so that he could admire her beauty at his leisure, especially her remarkable dark fleece, thick and curly, which complemented the velvety whiteness of her skin. Her resplendent blonde hair, which reached down to her waist, the lustre of her beautiful brown eyes, the sparkle of her teeth, and the heightened colour which every woman has just after making love – all these exquisite features offered to Claude's lingering gaze excited him to such a point that his virility, temporarily blunted by the sweet agony of pleasure he had just experienced under the prolonged oral stimulation of his friend, was quickly rekindled.

The young woman, delighted by this rapid renaissance, which is the sincerest compliment that a man can pay to a woman's charms, offered herself to her lover again, without restriction, so that he had the choice between her ravishing mound of Venus or the narrow retreat hidden between her firm young buttocks.

Claude's first preference was to explore this little hole because this was something new to him. Germaine explained to him what he should do and, turning round, knelt before him, her body bent forwards, her head buried in a pillow, parting her thighs for him and revealing the prettiest little arsehole imaginable. Claude, kneeling behind her, admired her splendid buttocks as he caressed them. He placed a globule of his saliva on the tiny orifice and, in order to facilitate penetration, another on the end of his swollen prick, then, parting her buttocks a little further with his hands, he placed his member against her narrow entrance, pushed gently forwards, and saw the full length of his rod slide slowly into her dilating anus until it disappeared. Germaine moved her backside back and forth gently and skilfully so that it was not long before Claude's member, gripped by her arse as if in a vice, ejaculated once again, squirting a fresh inundation of milky fluid into his lover's bowels, the constriction of the anus preventing him from draining himself in a single movement. At the same time the young man experienced the most exquisite sense of bliss which Germaine, as Claude had also been fondling her clitoris with his hand, entirely shared.

Claude generously thanked his friend for so kindly obliging him in this way. It was not until much later that he regained his own bedroom, and only after he had made the young woman climax yet again. This time, he had her in the same manner as Jean, the coachman, and his rod, thrust deep into Germaine's vagina, left a final and copious libation there. Lying on top of the naked body of his pretty mistress, mouth to mouth, tightly enlaced, they experienced once more the supreme delights of love-making.

Claude, who had grown rather fond of these charming games, wanted to repeat them as often as he could. He disported himself with the pretty maid, teasing her at all times of the day, tried to make love at the most inopportune moments in whichever room he accidentally stumbled across her, and even played one or two tricks on her of a rather mean nature.

Thus it was, one day, that finding Germaine leaning from a first floor window, talking with Claire and her sister, who were both in the garden, the absurd idea possessed him to have his way with her right then and there. Before she had time to realise what was going on, he had lowered the sash-window over the small of her back and closed the blinds. Then, hitching up her petticoats, and taking full advantage of the fact that she was completely trapped, he thrust his member into her vagina from behind at the same time as, slipping one of his hands round her front, he began to stroke and rub her clitoris. Despite her initial discontent, both on account of the inopportune nature of the attack and the fact that she was being taken from the rear, Germaine soon began to enjoy herself, wiggling her backside in the most provocative fashion; and Claude clearly heard the tinkling laughter of the two young girls outside, amazed at their maid's sudden stammer, her redness, how white her eyes had become, and the apparent loss of control she was suffering of her facial muscles while, unbeknown to them, she had an orgasm.

The innocent little dears did not for a single instant guess the real cause of Germaine's confusion, which they found so amusing, imagining that it was the consequence of a nervous reflex provoked by the fall of the window.

A YOUNG GIRL'S INITIATION

Germaine's natural inclination was towards women rather than men. Claire, with all her physical attractions, had made a powerful impression on her, but the girl's strict rule of chastity discouraged her and, one day, when she had tried to be overfamiliar with her mistress, placing her hand on her waist, she had been firmly put in her place. Circumstances had so directed events that she had had to end her special friendship with Claude, such that her attention slowly began to focus on Claire's younger sister.

Marguerite, whom we have so far only mentioned in passing, was an absolutely delightful girl of sixteen, with fragrant, beautifully groomed hair, as dark as that of her elder sister was fair, naturally wavy, which reached down to her shoulders where it provided a perfect backdrop, almost like a halo of chestnut, to the delicacy and paleness of her childlike face with its large, dark eyes, full of fun and intelligence, her crimson mouth, the very picture of innocence itself, and her tiny ears with their exquisitely formed folds.

Her shape, which was utterly perfect, was shown to good effect by her smock, which stopped at her knees, allowing the expensive embroidery of her knickers to stand out sharply, the whiteness of the linen contrasting with her black stockings, which moulded her finely sculpted calves.

Temperamentally, she was a happy, active girl, full of laughter and gaiety, always running and jumping; she was very girlish and utterly virginal; according to the rather common phrase, she looked as if butter wouldn't melt in her mouth. Cherished by all, everyone was free to stroke her beautifully brushed hair or place a kiss on her pink cheeks.

Germaine was naturally on more familiar terms with the girl than with her elder sister; Marguerite was not proud and could always be cajoled by the young maid whom she had adopted as her particular friend; in any case, her duties as chambermaid favoured such intimacy. Indeed, although she was not in the habit of undressing the girl ready for bed – Marguerite was quite of an age where she could do that for herself – she would undo for her the long row of buttons on her shoes. While this was happening, Marguerite would sit on the edge of her narrow bed, while her maid would squat at her feet. The girl would often lie back laughing on the bed as she moved her feet out of Germaine's reach. When she played this game, her short dress would ride up her body such that Germaine, whose eyes were on exactly the same level as the top of the bed, could clearly see all of Marguerite's underwear. She followed, from the knee as far as the hips, the plump thighs of the girl encased in their white knickers, fastened at the knee by a loop of lace, the transparency and slightly adhesive nature of the material clearly revealing the pink flesh beneath. Her lascivious gaze probed between the girl's thighs, coming to rest at the mysterious and intimate place of her sex, growing intoxicated on the warm effluvia and feminine odours which emanated from this region. Sometimes the girl's knickers were of the variety which does not possess an opening; but the attraction to her was no less powerful for all that, the stretch in the material as it passed over her flesh clearly modelling the girl's charming shape, the plump thighs, and the pubis; usually, though, she wore knickers with an opening. On those days, Germaine, extremely excited, would devour her intimate regions, hoping to spy during the course of Marguerite's sudden movements that charming sex of hers which attracted her so irresistibly, and occasionally glimpsing, in the very depths of her thighs, little corners of flesh redder than the others, and more elongated, the tiny sexual slit, just like a rosy pink mouth on which she would have liked to press her lips, lips avid to be kissed in return.

Germaine, in truth, steeled herself loyally to resist, certainly not out of virtue, but from fear of the consequences. What effect would an attempt, especially one which was a little too audacious, have on such an innocent girl? Did she not run the risk of being immediately reported to the girl's mother and shamefully given her notice? Is there not everything to be feared from a young girl? She awaited anxiously the onset of night, only too aware of the depths of her passion; but little by little she felt herself irresistibly lured on by her fatal desires. In order to prolong the lubricious spectacle which was vouchsafed her, she would tickle Marguerite in order to make her frolic

about and thus make her susceptible to her carnal gaze. She began by tickling her calves, then just behind the knee. Each day, she ventured a little further, stroking the outside of her thighs, then the inside. Moving upwards, she reached the waist, touching her tummy, hips, and armpits; sometimes her hand even brushed against her sexual parts, but she did not dare linger there. The girl twisted with laughter, her petticoats all dishevelled from the way she jumped about.

One evening, Marguerite noticed that the face of her maid had become extremely red and that she was staring hard under her skirt. Moreover, that very same day, Germaine, while pretending to tickle her thighs, had allowed her hand to brush against the girl's sexual parts, exposed through the opening in her knickers, more often than usual, so often, in fact, that there was something suspicious about the operation.

When her maid had retired, Marguerite thought over the meaning of her sudden discovery. Too innocent to work matters out for herself, she interrogated herself as to the cause of Germaine's excitation; slowly now she started to put two and two together. Marguerite recalled that, when she got out of the bath, her maid rubbed her with the towel through her peignoir more than was necessary between the thighs and the lower abdomen, something which had always embarrassed her. After having disrobed her of this soaking garment, Germaine often asked her to turn round while Marguerite, completely naked, did not want to reveal more than her back, out of prudery. Even before Marguerite had put on her chemise or knickers, Germaine made the girl sit down while she put stockings and shoes on her, and the maid was always opening her peignoir as if by accident; or again, when Marguerite went to play on the swing, Germaine would always be looking up under her skirt as she moved back and forth above her maid's head. These facts, which she had hardly noticed before, now seemed to take on a different meaning taken in conjunction. She finished by understanding and felt herself turning red, a little shamefully; she had never even dreamed of such a thing! She felt a sensation within her which was both very intense and yet indefinable. She was not vexed, far from it, there was nothing about this discovery which made her angry, her feelings were more those of astonishment and curiosity than anything else. What pleasure could there possibly be in looking at *that*, let alone touching it? How clever one is at sixteen! And how stupid she felt her maid was!

Nonetheless, she felt very excited herself and, after a moment's hesitation, she sat on a stool, in front of a candle, lifted up her skirt, and carefully studied, through the gap in her knickers, her sexual parts reflected in a mirror which she held in her hand. She thought their colour a pretty shade of red. Then she started to explore herself, parting her quim and probing it with her little finger, noting as she did so a slight swelling towards the top. After rubbing herself once or twice in this manner, she decided to go to bed, but slept badly. It all still seemed so extraordinary to her that she was unable to believe it and, in her imagination, she fixed upon a plan for the following day which would settle matters.

The next day, unable to contain herself until nightfall, she did indeed ring for her maid in the afternoon and asked her to change her shoes under the pretext that one of her feet hurt. Germaine did as she was requested, looking up at the girl's nether regions as was her custom, when she was astonished to see that Marguerite was not wearing any knickers. She threw herself back playfully on the bed, allowing her petticoats to ride even higher than was usual up her body, almost to the top of her thighs, which she held apart. Marguerite, red in the face at her own audacity, secretly studied her maid's face; this curiosity, which was now thoroughly awakened within her, was not without a certain pleasurable quality.

Germaine, turning suddenly pale and even a little embarrassed, stared steadily at the girl's body. Her blood rushed from her heart. This enchanting girlish nakedness, presented to her sight in full daylight, fascinated and intoxicated her; her desire to probe this velvety white flesh and to stroke her charming pink mound was intense; the temptation was too strong for her, she had no choice but to play her trump card. She tickled the legs and thighs of the girl in the normal way, just for the sake of appearances, then suddenly, completely overcome, she placed her hand over her sexual parts and left it there without moving it. Marguerite, mesmerised with wonder at what her maid was going to do next, remained as she was, laid back on the bed, with a beating heart; she felt her maid's trembling hand on her quim, which it timidly began to caress. A moment went by which seemed like an eternity. Germaine was studying the girl. Marguerite had still not uttered a word, done nothing to defend herself, even seemed to authorise, by her very passivity, the chambermaid's advances. The latter took courage and started to caress her in more active fashion until, tremendously excited herself by this stage, she abandoned all prudence and, wishing to resolve matters once and for all, she gently slipped her finger into Marguerite's slit and began to rub her little erect love button. Marguerite let all this happen as if in a trance, seeming not to realise what was being done to her. Germaine masturbated her more actively still and soon felt the little body jig up and down beneath her hands; the thighs of the girl squeezed together nervously and, as her breathing became faster and her skin grew flushed, she arched her back with pleasure at these new sensations even as, despite herself, she tried to dodge from Germaine's grasp and pull her skirt down over her legs. But the maid continued obstinately to rub her; and Marguerite felt the undiscovered heights of voluptuousness invade her body until, finally vanquished, she entirely abandoned herself between the young woman's arms, unconsciously opening her thighs wide apart. Germaine rolled her petticoats up over her stomach and surveyed the young girl's ravishing body, the white, slightly shiny stomach, where the blue course of her veins could be seen under the delicate skin, and her gorgeous quim, which was by now completely crimson.

Then, no longer able to control herself, she fell like a madwoman on the girl's sex, kissing it, taking it greedily between her lips in order to suck it. The most delicate of odours emanated from it, quite unique and utterly stimulating. Between her lips, Germaine could feel the swollen little clitoris, and this is where she focused her attention, teasing it and licking it with the full length of her tongue. The girl writhed under such voluptuous caresses, squeezing Germaine's head between her thighs and jerking backwards, her entire body stiff, and her breathing laboured; then she reached the final spasm and, inundating the maid's face, she fell back exhausted by her first encounter with such extraordinary pleasure.

Once her excitement had worn off, Germaine expected that the girl would burst into tears and lamentations. To her astonishment, this was not the case; Marguerite was still too innocent to understand fully what had happened to her virginal body. What she found most surprising was that her maid had pressed her mouth against that particular part of her body. She thought to herself that it was a horrible thing to do, and the predominant feeling she had was one of shame. Scarlet with embarrassment, her head in her hands, her short dress pulled down chastely over her knees and squeezed between her legs, Marguerite remained a long time like that without daring to look at Germaine and without uttering a single word.

As for the maid, she too had come to her senses, and realised just how dangerous her situation was, how close she was to losing her position and perhaps suffering even more severe penalties. There was only one thing for it: to dispel the memory of what had just happened by becoming close friends with the girl herself. She helped Marguerite to her feet, took her ravishing head with its long chestnut hair between her hands, and covered her warm cheeks, lowered eyes and mouth, which was damp and as soft as satin, with passionate kisses, whispering in her ear in a low voice and trying to make her smile.

'If only you knew how I love you, my darling little Marguerite; how pretty you are, and what a beautiful body you have, it must have been made to be kissed and caressed.'

'Oh, Germaine, I am so ashamed; I can't even look at you.'

'Don't be silly! There is nothing unusual about what has happened. How often have I seen you without any clothes on? And as you are my own very special friend, I wanted to kiss you as gently as I could to give you pleasure.'

'I know that, but why did you have to kiss me there? I can't get over what you did. I have always been told never to lift my skirt, and if mother sometimes insists that I wear knickers without an opening in them, it can only be so that people can't see my... well, you know exactly what I mean.'

'Of course, my sweet; but now that I have seen it, no damage has been done.'

'I had no idea that people did such dirty things as

that.'

'But it's not at all dirty.'

'Germaine! How could you put your mouth in a place where one…'

'Where one passes water? But it is such a tender spot, and there are no consequences whatsoever, as long as no one knows about it. And think how much pleasure it gives, as you know yourself; do you think I didn't spot how you were bucking up and down in my arms moaning with pleasure?'

'But Germaine!'

'You were writhing around in pleasure, you were squeezing my head between your thighs fit to suffocate me!'

'But Germaine!'

'And when it was all over, you threw yourself backwards with a little scream, and I felt my mouth completely inundated with your juices.'

'Oh!'

And gently moving away the hands with which the girl was hiding herself, Germaine kissed her with infinite tenderness on the mouth, looking at her closely, eye to eye. Then she said to her in a low voice:

'Tell me, my little darling, did you feel any pleasure?'

The girl, still blushing furiously, could not help smiling at the intimacy of the question; she looked at the maid without anger and, after a brief hesitation, she leaned forward and whispered in her ear:

'Yes!'

'A lot of pleasure? Pleasure is good for you, you know.'

'Oh, yes! I liked it very much!'

And she looked at Germaine, her face brightening up, with gratitude in her eyes for the immense, and entirely new to her, pleasure which the maid had caused her to experience, and also for the great discovery she had made, a discovery which, she vaguely realised, would lead to all kinds of other voluptuous delights in the future.

Germaine, while still continuing to hug her tenderly and cajole her, softly slipped her hand below the girl's waist, exploring, almost without her realising it, between her thighs until it reached the sexual slit which was still extremely damp.

'Would you show me, my darling, how much you love me and that you are really not vexed with me for teaching you these new things? Let me stroke your delicious mound and make you come once more. Will you let me do this, my dear?'

'Oh, Germaine! Yes, please!'

Marguerite looked at her, blushing once again, still hesitant, then she slipped her arms around the maid's neck and put her mouth against her ear:

'Oh, yes, please!'

Germaine began to caress the girl again. Marguerite, aroused once more, abandoned herself as she squeezed herself against the maid. As soon as she felt Germaine expertly rubbing her clitoris, which was already very excited, her entire body was racked with a nervous tremor and she began to breathe unevenly. Soon her thighs started to squeeze together, she hugged the maid with her slender arms, and her body began to arch. Germaine, leaning over her, stared avidly into the depths of her eyes, seeking to chart the progress of the girl's orgasm. Thrilling at the sight of the gentle Marguerite's pleasure, she drank in her panting breath and wiped the saliva from her mouth with her own lips. Her senses excited to the very highest pitch by the sensuality of such a sight, she squeezed her own thighs with frenzy, realising that she would not be able to stop herself coming at any moment.

She masturbated Marguerite's erect little clitoris faster than ever as she saw her eyes begin to loll, but the girl soon closed her eyelids, from that instinctive *pudeur* which comes at the moment of orgasm, and which she could now feel was upon her, making her entire body tremble, and forcing her to utter cries of pleasure.

Germaine, in the sway of a violent and irresistible desire to come herself, fell across the bed, hitching up her dress above the hips before the surprised and curious eyes of the little girl who had never before seen a woman with such luxuriant pubic hair. The young woman procured for herself the same delights that she had shown to Marguerite, who noted with the greatest attention what actions Germaine made in order to pleasure herself, and followed with passionate interest every stage of the voluptuous chambermaid's orgasm.

VIRTUE AT BAY

What's bred in the bone will come out in the flesh, or so said the poet. This is above all true when what is bred in the bone comes clothed with all the natural enthusiasm and passion of youth. Of course, Claude had been quite truthful with Claire at the moment of their reconciliation, but he was anything but sincere as he caved in to the irresistible temptations of the flesh. His easy conquest of the pretty chambermaid did nothing to diminish his desire for Claire; on the contrary, their lecherous antics kept his senses continually on edge such that he was forever haunted by the urge to possess the virginal body of his ravishing friend. Since the scene in the bedroom, to which he had never since made the slightest allusion, the young man had not taken any steps capable of troubling the girl's sense of prudery, although this was mainly because circumstances had so far not proved favourable, but such a state of affairs could not endure forever.

Claude had experienced the resistance that the young girl made to any unwelcome advance on his part. She would immediately pull herself away from her lover's amorous embrace, thus making any attack impossible. What he would have liked to do was to take her senses unawares and, in some way or another, transmit the sensation of sexual arousal to her. But in order to make this happen it was necessary to find a place where Claire had no chance of making any resistance, as had once, all too briefly, already been the case. But he had to admit to himself that such an unlikely set of circumstances were not going to happen of their own accord. However, his lucky star so arranged matters that a short time later this is precisely what did occur.

Towards the end of June, a letter informed the inhabitants of the château that M. and Mme de Messange, who had been dipping their toes in the Parisian high life, as they did each year around the time of the Grand Prix, were coming home. It was immediately decided that they would all go together to meet them at the station at Verneuil. Their neighbour, Mme d'Estange, with her open carriage, would also join the party. But hardly had they started out before the rain started to bucket down with such force that everyone had to take shelter in the closed barouche of the Messanges. The old carriage was unequal to such an honour, and one and all had to squeeze and huddle together as best they could.

Claude cunningly seated Claire on his knee, holding her around the waist to prevent her from wriggling free. This position, rather an unbecoming one for a girl of her age, made everybody laugh, but as there was more room for the others this way, no one made any objection, and even Claire resigned herself to the situation.

The rain soon stopped, but the sky was still full of clouds, and the interior of the carriage was half in darkness. No one spoke a word as they were all under the melancholic spell of this peaceful summer's evening.

As for our young lover though, a completely different sensation had seized hold of him, invading his entire body until it possessed the very seat of his being. His beautiful friend was there on his knee, and he was totally surrounded by the odour emanating from her glorious blonde hair as it cascaded down over her neck, which he greedily nuzzled. He could feel her breath on his face as she moved her head slightly and the heat radiated by her slender, young body. Hidden under her coat, his trembling hands feverishly caressed Claire's stomach. His excitement must have communicated itself to the young girl, because he could feel the sudden movement of her breasts and her sudden intakes of breath. The poor creature realised that she was entirely at Claude's mercy and that she could do nothing whatsoever to stop him from touching her in those places that most offended her modesty!

Claude, too, had reached the same conclusion and, mad with desire, he gave himself free range to caress her in the most intimate manner. Having surreptitiously slipped his right hand beneath his beautiful burden, he had quickly found a way into the light summer dress and through the satin under-skirt she was wearing; then he had gently groped his way forward to discover whether there was an opening into her knickers. He eventually found one into which he could insert his hand, and he could feel, through the delicate linen of her camisole, the warmth of her youthful sexual parts.

From the very outset, Claire had counted herself for lost. What could she do? How could she arrest Claude's progress? She knew that the least word of protest on her part would attract the attention of everyone sitting opposite her, and the thought that they might see what was going on made her want to die of shame. She could feel Claude as he slowly edged the tails of her camisole out of the way and, sliding his hand between her totally naked thighs, had now reached her vagina. The poor girl whispered imploringly in his ear:

'Please, no! I would love you all the more if you would only remove your hand!'

At the same time, she tried to protect herself, squeezing her thighs together as tightly as she could, so imprisoning the hand of the young man where it was. But the girl's sexual parts had now become moist as a result of the intensity of the emotion she was experiencing, and despite her stubborn resistance, Claude managed to slip his finger between the lips of her sex and so attain the hard, swollen button of her clitoris. With an infinite gentleness, he caressed and teased it, before turning his attention to the exploration of her slit, only to return once more to the centre of her sexual longings which he could feel tingling under his finger. And he prolonged these delicious caresses – sometimes gently, and at other times briskly – masturbating the girl whose laboured breathing and nervous spasms he could now feel, as her hands gripped the carriage upholstery. Claire had ceased defending herself. From time to time, she squeezed her thighs together uncontrollably before opening them wide, unintentionally aiding Claude's activities. She was seized by a feeling impossible to describe. The young man could clearly see that his delicate labours by no means left his friend indifferent and that, for the first time in her life, she was at last allowing herself to be dominated by the sensation of sensual pleasure. This observation only served to excite him all the more, and he redoubled the movement of his fingers against her slit, which was now extremely wet, and passionately masturbated her erect little clitoris. This game could not go on unpunished for long: suddenly, he felt his hand being covered in a warm liquid, while Claire, almost fainting, sprawled over him, while trying to grab the side of the carriage. Except for Marguerite, who was sitting next to her sister, no one noticed this incident. Out of the corner of her eye, the young girl had been following every development, and understood exactly what Claude was doing, but she had not breathed a word. A few moments later and the carriage arrived at its destination.

Claire had still not recovered from this awakening of her senses, an awakening which had had such a startling effect on her, she was still affected by the time she retired to her bedroom that evening. A temperament as warm as hers, a trait which ran in the family, as we have seen with regard to her younger sister, could not help but feel such pleasures more keenly than others, and her climax had been of a most violent nature.

All her illusions were shattered; she no longer knew what to believe. The revelation had been so sudden, so unexpected, and above all so intense! She undressed slowly, dreaming to herself, knowing full well that it was unlikely that she would be able to sleep that night. She wanted to see the body that so excited her old schoolboy chum and, forgetting her usual prudery, allowed to fall, one after the other, all the veils which covered her until, for the first time, she saw herself naked in the mirror.

Beautiful? Oh, yes, she was beautiful! She recognised the fact with a sense of indefinable pleasure. She examined herself feature by feature both by sight and by hand: the firm, exquisitely-shaped breasts, the clean lines of the hips, which emphasised her slender, well-proportioned physique, the soft flesh of the buttocks, the flawless silhouette of her stomach. She did not even avert her gaze from her curly, blonde pubis which half-concealed the pink lips of her temple of love... Even though she could feel herself blushing, she wanted to see everything! She turned round and admired her back, the curve of her spine, and her pretty little bottom with its firm, rounded buttocks, the cheeks as smooth and radiant as pearls with just a suggestion of pinkness about their summits as on her face. Then, with the help of a hand-mirror, she examined with ever greater attention her grotto of love, gently parting the lips which concealed the entrance, seeking to become familiar with this intimate recess.

She wondered whether she had not become the sport of a dream, whether all that had happened was real, whether the searing pleasure she had experienced was not the product of her own over-stimulated imagination. How to tell? Even so, she would hardly dare to... And she put down the mirror in order to go to sleep, but she was irresistibly drawn back to it, and her hand, as if of its own volition, slipped between her thighs where, utterly confused as she was, she began to play with herself again just as Claude had done with her earlier. How true it was! She experienced the same pleasurable sensations as she had done before! Her hand began to move more rapidly and focused its attention on the upper part of her sex, the place where she felt the sharpest stabs of pleasure. She experienced the same giddiness, the same delicious sensation which spread throughout her entire body. In her quest for knowledge, the gentle Claire learned so quickly and so expertly that she tottered, half-fainting, in an armchair, her body racked by an orgasm that happened so quickly that she heard herself cry out as she felt her hand become wet.

During the following days, she maintained a discreet reserve with regard to her friend, whom she did her best to avoid. Claude understood that she was not really angry with him; the dominant emotion which ruled her was rather more one of shame. As if by tacit agreement, there was no mention by either of them of what had taken place in the carriage. Claude, thoroughly enchanted at the tremendous strides he had made at imparting to his friend a knowledge of the pleasures of the senses, had no intention of hurrying matters.

A PRECOCIOUS GIRL;
THE YOUNG LADIES' ACADEMY

Marguerite made the most of the instruction she received at the hands of her maid, for the seed had fallen on fertile ground; she had become the most passionate girl you can possibly imagine. Soon, Germaine no longer sufficed as partner in her erotic games, she had set her heart on Claude. The lubricious scene in the carriage had stuck in her memory; burning as she was with desire to be caressed by the handsome young man, she had spoken about this neither to her sister nor to her maid. She was fascinated by the idea of the male member; she wanted to know all about this organ, about which Germaine had told her, and above all to see one close-up and to be able to touch it at her leisure. Marguerite was a cunning little minx, and she thought she saw a way of turning the occasional lessons in gymnastics which she had with Claude to her advantage. The gymnasium was to be found on the first floor of the château, at the end of one of the wings. Claude would call for the girl when he had some spare time, and the lessons, which were quite short, generally took place without anyone else being present.

In her determination to make her plan work, Marguerite spared no effort to inflame the young man. Despite the formal instructions of her mother, she no longer wore knickers of the enclosed variety. Standing upright with one foot in each of the suspended rings, which he held steady beneath her, the girl moved her legs as far apart as they would go, leaving the young man in a state of utter confusion at the sight of her exposed lower body. His lascivious gaze, which immediately strayed to the place between her thighs, was not even hindered by the cloth of her knickers, for in this position, the opening fell agape of its own accord, thus revealing the intimate parts they were expressly designed to conceal from indiscreet eyes.

Or else she would take the rings in her hands in order to complete a somersault, but she would stop in the middle with her head facing towards the ground and her feet in the air. Dress, petticoats, everything would tumble down, covering her face, while her legs, thighs and stomach were left completely exposed. And even in this position she would straddle her legs in order that Claude could see through the opening in her knickers that little slit which she knew he was desperate to study, especially when he thought there was not the slightest chance of being surprised in this occupation.

In the same way she also exercised on the trapeze, suspending herself using the bend of her knees, with her head swinging towards the ground, or on the rope ladder, which he would hold from beneath her, while she would jig up and down above him, trying to catch his head in the folds of her skirts.

Claude would not have been the young man he was if he had not been aroused by these little games of seduction which is what he eventually decided they

were. Marguerite, as we have already said, was extremely well-behaved and, with her dark hair which fell in graceful curls over her shoulders, as pretty as a picture. It was only the fear of the girl letting slip indiscretions that caused him to hesitate.

Marguerite saw clearly how his eyes shone with desire, and how he was so aroused that his voice trembled in the funniest manner during their gymnastics lessons, and she was vexed when he remained bashful with her.

Remembering the tactics she had employed so successfully with the maid, she decided to bring matters to a head. One day she asked to be excused for a few moments during the course of her lesson: Claude imagined that she needed to answer a call of nature. When she returned, she was somewhat flushed and embarrassed; she climbed back on the rings where she had been exercising her legs, then, requesting the young man to watch over her as she tried out a new exercise, she threw back her head and suspended herself using the bend of her knees.

The sight that greeted Claude's eyes aroused him to fever pitch: her petticoats fell over her head, leaving all her intimate parts completely naked, from the garters holding up her black stockings above the knee to her waist. One cannot imagine anything more adorable than the charming body of this dark-haired girl: her dimpled thighs, finely sculpted and of an unsullied whiteness; the perfectly flat stomach with its skin as smooth and velvety as that of a peach and so transparent that all the little blue veins running in every direction just below the surface could be plainly distinguished; her firm, slender buttocks, between which could be glimpsed a microscopically small pink hole with the most delicate crinkles around it, the general effect being that this was the most graceful little arsehole imaginable; and between her thighs those two adorable little lips, as red as cherries and flawless in every detail, in whose midst was hidden the tiny organ of love which was just crying out to be kissed. Obviously, the lascivious little minx had left the room in order to remove her knickers, which she had been wearing at the beginning of the class! This was too much for the professor's virtue. Gripped by an irresistible desire, Claude threw himself like a madman on the girl's body which he carried to a sofa, pressing his lips between her thighs, in exactly the same place as her sex, kissing it, sucking it, and passing his tongue all along her slit, rubbing her already erect clitoris until the moment when the girl, who was writhing convulsively in his hands and arching her back in the most provocative manner, arrived at the blissful moment of orgasm and fell into a faint.

Claude had hardly recovered from his emotion when Marguerite, in a slightly embarrassed tone, asked in a low voice if she could see his sex in turn. As he hesitated to reply to such an unforeseen question, the precocious minx squatted between his legs and began to undo the buttons on his breeches. She managed, not without some difficulty, to liberate his erect member.

She was enraptured by this new object which she had

never encountered before, holding the testicles and rolling them in her hand, stroking the entire length of the rod which reared up nervously under her slim fingers. She covered and uncovered the crimson head, astonished by the thickness of the veins swelling under the surface; finally, she held it in both hands and began to rub it back and forth. This game was the cause of a little misadventure which she was far from expecting: when Claude's love liquid finally spurted out, she received a discharge full in the face.

The young man remained extremely uneasy about these goings-on given the serious nature of the probable consequences; and he was only too pleased when, a few weeks later, Marguerite was sent off to finish her education at a boarding-school in Orléans.

The girl took all her precocious sexual habits with her to this new environment, where she quickly found suitable subjects in the form of her classmates. In the schoolroom, in the dormitories, in the bath-house, she found ample opportunity to give free rein to her pleasures, either alone or with the other girls who, though timid enough to begin with, soon took a singular delight in such occupations and gave themselves up to them wholeheartedly.

Her greatest pleasure was to creep about during class under the tables which served the pupils as desks. There, she would slip between the legs of one of the girls whom she found particularly attractive, push up her skirt and, through the gap in her knickers, caress her sexual parts, sometimes kissing and licking them. The victim of this exercise would not dare to object from fear of attracting the mistress's attention.

Thus it was that one day an absolutely ravishing, and entirely innocent, seventeen-year-old called Jeanne caught sight of her performing such an act on her neighbour and immediately began to feel extremely aroused. It happened like this. Jeanne, busy writing, noticed that the bench on which she was sitting had begun to vibrate in an annoying manner; looking round to discover the reason for this, she was amazed by the behaviour of the girl to her right.

The girl was moving agitatedly on the bench; her breath was irregular and wheezy, and her face red to the roots of her hair; her lips had become damp and her beautiful dark eyes, also glistening, betrayed an indefinable expression of pleasure: a sort of bliss seemed to emanate from her entire being. All the girls around her, who were watching this scene unfold avidly, were exchanging smiles and other signs of intelligence, but discreetly, so as not to attract the attention of the mistress; they seemed to derive some sort of wicked pleasure from this spectacle, even though they did not seem to find it particularly unusual. Jeanne, intrigued, bent down to see what was happening under the table. What she saw awoke the most incredible feelings in the innocent girl; Marguerite was squatting under the table, balancing on her heels, with her knees wide apart. In this position, her short skirt no longer covered her body, and through the opening in her knickers it was possible to see all her sexual parts. Meanwhile, Marguerite held up as far out of reach as possible the skirt and petticoats of her neighbour, while her right hand, which reached between her thighs, made a gentle rubbing motion in a place which, though Jeanne knew all about it, nonetheless made her blush with embarrassment. The eroticism of this scene, though it explained to Jeanne the reason for her neighbour's visible emotion, caused in her a sense of astonishment not far from stupefaction; matters had been going on like this for some minutes when Marguerite suddenly thrust her head between the girl's thighs, letting her skirt and petticoats fall over her as she did so, such that nothing more was to be seen. Jeanne raised her eyes to look at her neighbour. Marguerite's sudden movement had plunged her into a most unusual condition: her breath came out in gasps, her eyes dilated with pleasure, she stretched her legs out under the table and rubbed them against each other involuntarily, such that they threatened to suffocate the lascivious girl; her fists clenched nervously; her entire body experienced a state of bliss close to ecstasy. Several times she tried to struggle free of the carnal embrace, but in vain. Finally, a last voluptuous spasm shook the girl's body and she slumped back in her chair. Marguerite quickly moved back, rubbing her sleeve over the lower part of her mouth as if to dry it; then, without making the slightest sound, using her hands and her knees, she regained her own place with all the agility of a cat.

An emotion just as intense was in store for young Jeanne. That very evening, in the dormitory, as all the

other girls slept while she was kept awake by the
memory of the lubricious scene she had witnessed that
afternoon and which had thrown her into a state of
utter confusion, she saw Marguerite approach her bed,
bend down affectionately so that her head with its long
dark curls was almost next to hers, and beg to have a
turn at pleasuring her.

This request, unexpected as it was, plunged Jeanne
into an inexplicable state of turmoil. What she had seen
earlier had tremendously excited her, provoking a lust in
her which was almost brutal; lured on by such an
invincible curiosity, she allowed Marguerite to kiss her
on the mouth while her experienced hand already
strayed under her chemise, stroking her naked body and
seeking out the secret places. The brave blonde girl still
tried to resist and to shake off these luxurious caresses,
but in vain, she was soon vanquished. In the blink of an
eye, Marguerite had stretched herself out on the bed
next to her, but in the opposite direction, that is to say
with her legs towards the pillow and her head towards
the foot of the bed. Throwing back the bedclothes and
hitching up Jeanne's chemise, she examined her
beautiful virginal body, unsullied by the slightest
contact, with the greatest pleasure, allowing her
lecherous hand to dally all over it lovingly, even visiting
the most hidden corners, which caused the most intense
sensations in her. In fact, both girls were equally moved
by what was happening. Soon, Jeanne felt Marguerite's
warm, damp tongue audaciously exploring her lower
abdomen and the inside of her thighs, pretending to kiss

her. Then suddenly, as if shedding all sense of shame, and after looking at her friend in supplication, Marguerite, blushing all over, applied her lips to the fire raging in the young girl's sexual parts and Jeanne's stomach arched with pleasure under this delicate caress, her body jerking backwards, and, with her eyes closed, she felt herself invaded by a blissful intoxication.

When she opened her eyes, she was surprised to find the naked body of Marguerite pressed against her face, with her chemise pulled up over her stomach as a result of her movements. Her body was absolutely adorable. The fair-haired girl examined avidly the dimpled thighs and the exquisite lines of her stomach. The dark pubescent down cast a shadow over her lower body, contrasting strongly with the marble whiteness of her skin.

Between her thighs could be seen the two lips, red and damp with excitement, from which an entirely sexual odour emanated. This sight, together with what she had already experienced under the luxurious caresses of Marguerite, was enough to make Jeanne lose her head. Overwhelmed by such voluptuousness, and becoming giddy with desire, she threw herself on the naked body of Marguerite, squeezing her in her arms as if she wanted to suffocate her and covering with burning kisses her pale thighs, her stomach, but above all the crimson quim which opened as if by magic when she breathed on it. She licked the clitoris ardently, swollen and red as it was. Marguerite's entire body quivered under her touch; panting, and racked by nervous spasms, she writhed with pleasure. A final spasm of utter bliss, one which made her cry out with pleasure, shook the body of the dark-haired girl and a warm dew dampened Jeanne's lips before she had time to pull her head away. At the same moment, she too was reaching the ultimate stages of pleasure, and she fell back against her pillow, intoxicated with pleasure.

These scenes were often repeated with an infinite variety of refinements. Marguerite was truly gifted at initiating the young girls with whom she boarded in these delightful games of love, games in which everyone was only too willing to seek instruction, such that when she returned to the Château de Messanges for the summer holidays there was hardly a single pupil in her class whose little anus she had not played with or a clitoris she had not masturbated while blissfully licking the quim.

LOVE VANQUISHES ALL

This sudden exposure to the pleasures of the flesh marked a veritable turning point in the life of Claude's charming friend. A nature as lively and warm as that of Claire, full of every feminine curiosity, could not but be profoundly marked by a discovery as unsettling as this one.

The poor young girl was utterly disoriented; she could not get over it and was completely prostrate as a result, knowing full well as she did that in her present state of moral upheaval she was at the young man's mercy should he renew his attack on her. All her instinctive chastity, the virtuous nature of her soul which had protected her until that moment, was impotent faced with the haunting memory of such burning pleasures, pleasures repeated on numerous occasions subsequently; for, at those times when one's will-power is sapped by the onset of sleep, and even at other moments when entirely conscious, the young girl had not been able to restrain her hand from straying to the place which had been so keenly stimulated by Claude. Each time, her caresses had resulted in an increasingly intense sensation of pleasure, such that her need for stimulation, a need which is perhaps latent in the female sexual organs, grew from day to day. Indeed, Claire was in such an overexcited state, both mentally and physically, that she, as virtuous and pure as she was, actually looked forward to Claude making such an approach. The hand of a man, she admitted to herself, especially the hand of a man she loved as ardently as Claude, would take her to new heights of physical and emotional bliss, heights far greater than any pleasure she would be able to procure by her own amateurish auto-erotic activity. But Claude was now in full retreat, not daring to risk his earlier success by returning to the attack too soon; and, however great her own desire, she would have died of shame before taking any steps to encourage her friend to return to the charge.

Claude too was well aware of the young girl's mounting emotions while, for him, his frustration had reached such a stage that he felt that the dénouement could not be far off and that the least thing could provoke it.

And, in fact, this dénouement, so ardently desired by the two youngsters, but which neither of them dared to bring about of their own volition, was eventually brought about by pure chance.

One afternoon Claire had withdrawn into a tiny summer house in the grounds of the park in order to escape the heat of the day; giving free rein to the thoughts which preoccupied her, she had stretched herself out nonchalantly on a deep sofa which was the only furniture in the room; almost certainly she was about to engage in some solitary caresses when, by good fortune, Claude happened to wander in with the intention of having a rest. At this sudden apparition, all the blood rushed from her heart, and she understood that the moment she both desired and dreaded had arrived. Her first thought had been to flee, but now that the time had come her passion proved to be so great that not only did she stay but also, closing her eyes, she resolved that she would pretend to be asleep, in order to give the young man free rein to do with her exactly what she hoped he would do but dared not ask of him.

The intensity of her emotion made her heart beat faster and caused her breath to become short and erratic; laid out on her back, her eyes closed and her face flushed, she pretended as best she was able to be asleep. Tortured by anxiety at the same time as in the grips of an unassailable desire, she felt the young man gradually creep towards her and lift her skirt and petticoat as far as her waist... Then his fingers slowly strayed up her thighs until they attained the mysterious forest. But her legs must have been too close together for Claude to satisfy his ardent curiosity, for she felt him move them apart with an infinite tenderness so as not to wake her. Finally, he pulled apart the opening in her knickers and carefully pulled up her chemise.

For her to know that her most intimate parts had been fully exposed to the young man's gaze and to realise that she was entirely at his mercy was a sensation that can scarcely be described.

For a moment, which seemed like a century, she felt him examining her, then she trembled at the contact of his hand which brushed lightly over her little quim with its damp lips, moving from top to bottom, but above all playing with the tiny mound just below her pubis. But

soon her excitation increased further still; Claude, who had slipped between her thighs, was ardently flicking his tongue over her most intimate parts; he licked her adorable vulva and all the folds of skin around it, sucked the pretty lips which he caught in his mouth, and fell upon her adorable button of love, which was very developed in Claire's case, and which he bit with all the passionate frenzy of a rutting animal which, after being long denied the object of its affection, has just been set free and is in a state of erotic intoxication.

In fact, Claude seemed to have lost any sense of prudence, any fear of waking the young girl. Mad with passion, he had seized her thighs with both hands, ripping off her knickers which were getting in his way, and he licked her sex with what was almost fury, his tongue burning with desire; his hands fondled the adorable girl's buttocks voluptuously, which squirmed uncontrollably under this luxurious embrace and the movement of his tongue, both sensations entirely new to her. A delirious wave of pleasure shook her entire body; she had reached her climax and was in the throes of a spasm of such erotic intensity that she lost any sensation of reality and which made her cry out aloud in veritable ecstasy.

Claude raised his head and their eyes met... he read in them her utter abandonment of all resistance... The adorable young girl, in the transports of love and drunk with voluptuousness, yielded herself completely to him. With eyes full of gratitude and an ineffable tenderness, she pulled Claude towards her and gave his mouth a long, loving kiss. Then, in a moment of wild, animal-like lust, he ripped open his fly buttons, behind which his prick was imprisoned, and lodged it in the entrance of the girl's virginal chamber while wrapping his entire body around her and showering her gracious face with kisses; Claire, herself excited beyond measure, entirely abandoned herself to him, parting her thighs of her own volition, though she hardly understood what her friend intended to do. Claude had not stopped pressing his rod into Claire's grotto of love, still damp from her previous climax, a circumstance which would favour the actual penetration. Then, feeling his erect member slide into the tight little opening, and squeezing his friend hard in his arms while pressing his burning lips against hers, he leaned heavily against her, bursting through the fragile barrier of virginity with a couple of thrusts of his hips, so penetrating right into the heart of the temple of love. Claire, surprised to feel suddenly a sharp pain, cried out so loudly that the sound was only just muffled by her lover's lips, and tears formed in her eyes despite herself; she felt a burning sensation in the same place that she had earlier experienced nothing but an overwhelming voluptuousness, and she imagined she had been injured. But, almost right away, she felt Claude begin to move faster, hold her more passionately in his arms, press his lips more firmly against her, and a spasm of extraordinary intensity shook her entire body, while his manhood squirted into the very depths of her being a hot liquid which immediately began to soothe her pain.

The act of possession, which had begun so long ago

and been awaited with such anticipation, had finally been consummated.

And Claude now spoke to her softly of love, consoling and embracing her tenderly, reassuring her, explaining the nature of the act of love to her and the inevitable pain, and thanking her for the tremendous joy that she had just given him.

Claire, trusting in him and regaining heart, quickly dried her tears and each sought to enrapture the other with delightful promises of eternal love.

Claude got up and delicately wiped away the drops of blood which adorned the entrance to the beautiful grotto, which was now available to all love's pleasures; he kissed the delicate flesh, still trembling with emotion, and gazed avidly at his friend's secret charms. Claire willingly allowed him to do this and, in her turn, wanted to explore her lover's body; she held the instrument which had made a woman of her in her hand and studied it curiously; she stroked the round balls which she rolled between her fingers. Most of all she was fascinated by the virile member. She admired the fineness of the little veins which rippled under the skin, the suppleness of the hood which she gently pushed back, discovering the gland with its small opening at the end. As a result of being touched in this way, the organ of love soon became erect again, proudly raising up its ruby-coloured head, ready once more for love's combat. Enchanted and excited at the same time, the young girl wanted to feel what it was like to be penetrated a second time by this splendid rod, and despite the slight burning sensation which she could still feel, she drew Claude into her arms and said:

'Would you like to do it again?'

Claude's only reply was to squeeze her against his heart and kiss her madly on the mouth; then, altering his position, he pulled Claire towards him after removing her dress and petticoat which were getting in his way.

And obedient pupil that she was, Claire lent herself to his fancy. Following his instructions, she straddled herself across his waist, her legs bent at the knees on each side; Claude gently eased his member into the tight passage, which was still hurting from her previous encounter, and, beckoning her towards him, he made her lean forwards, her lips against his, while with his hand, which he slipped between her thighs, he stroked her erect clitoris. Claire, in the throes of pleasure and forgetting her earlier pain, began to move her body, thus rubbing against the hardened rod which penetrated her. Before long she felt herself swooning with pleasure while her vagina was inundated with a warm and copious ejaculation.

For the first time together, the two lovers experienced in each other's arms the most indescribable pleasures, culminating with, in the form of a final spasm, the delicious sensations of love.

Prudence demanded that these intoxicating revels eventually drew to a close, however. Becoming more serious again, they got dressed, and Claude, who understood the danger that the act of love could occasion for his friend, namely an unforeseen pregnancy, explained to her the precautions which she should take.

Radiant with love and pleasure, just like Daphnis and Chloe after their initiation, the two youngsters kissed each other tenderly, promised each other eternal happiness and slowly made their way back to the château.

THE ENTIRE GAMUT OF EMOTIONS!

The discovery of the act of love was for Claire the starting point of a complete transformation of her character and ideas. She no longer recognised herself. Once so shy and reserved, she was now continually troubled by an indefinable longing at the merest thought of sexual pleasure, thoughts towards which she was irresistibly drawn by her exceptionally ardent temperament, a temperament which had been fully awakened and excited to the highest pitch. This was all she could think about, this new pleasure which was so intense, and she was astonished to note how quickly that sense of shame she used to feel when in Claude's arms had disappeared.

The blonde young girl would have liked to abandon herself utterly to her gentle lover; but she understood that extreme prudence was required if she was not to lose her beloved Claude, and this difficulty was for her but another spur. The park, with its shady trees, offered the two lovers a suitable haven to exchange their vows of love out of reach of indiscreet ears and to exchange little kisses and cuddles; but the summer house would hardly suffice for their love frolics, and they decided to meet every night in Claude's bedroom which, since it was in a distant part of the château, represented the safest place of refuge.

The day after the memorable events that had taken

place in the summer house, while the inhabitants of the château slumbered in their beds, Claire, dressed only in her peignoir and slippers, made her way to her lover's room where she was awaited.

No sooner had she arrived and they were in each other's arms. 'There you are at last, my beloved Claire!' said Claude, squeezing her against him as he looked into the pretty eyes, damp with desire, and kissed them. Such an emotion made Claire even more beautiful. Happy to have her lover to herself once again, she kissed him in her turn, and their lips united in a long, tender kiss, a kiss in which they each placed their entire soul.

Claude could feel the lithe body of his pretty little mistress, protected only by her peignoir, pressed against him. How he loved that body, which he had done little more than glimpse the day before. He knew how perfect it was though, and he wanted to discover every detail about it.

'Oh! Claire! How sweet you are!' he told her. 'I can feel your heart beat next to mine, I can feel your firm, upright breasts against my chest; but your charms are concealed from me, my dear. I want to see everything, worship your pretty body, without anything being hidden from me. Will you do this for me?'

'Yes, my dearest Claude, in order to please you, I shall do everything you ask.'

And Claude removed her peignoir and slippers and made her chemise fall to the ground. Then he contemplated the ravishingly beautiful naked body of the young girl; his eyes wide with ecstasy showed the extent of his admiration. Claire, delighted by her lover's joy, revealed everything to his eyes, smiling and complaisant, turning round as he required to show off her marvellous back and buttocks. And Claude provided a commentary out loud as she did so:

'How beautiful you are like that, my little Clairette! Your skin is soft and pale; your breasts are ravishing, see how they are already fully grown, firm and supple in my hand, look how the pink spots of your little nipples stand erect for me. I can see the blue veins running under the transparent skin of your pretty stomach; your hips are perfectly formed, just like your bottom; one could not even dream of a prettier one, with its plump, healthy cheeks.'

'Me, too,' said Claire. 'I would like to see you. I shall undress you myself.'

And she quickly removed his pyjama trousers and nightshirt so that she in her turn could admire this well-proportioned body; but her gaze soon passed to his erect penis, and her hands immediately began to caress and stroke this proud instrument of love.

Then the young man swept his mistress off the ground in his arms and deposited her on the bed; he covered her in the wildest kisses and caresses. His hands delicately massaged the beautiful body before him, with its erect nipples, its dimpled thighs, and its sensitive stomach; his agile fingers brushed her beautiful temple of love. Then, turning Claire over, he stroked her neck, her back as smooth as silk, and her plump little buttocks, which he gently parted in order to tickle the slit in between them and the delicious rose hidden within; then his movements became faster, more determined, and her pretty bottom began to turn red from being stroked and kneaded.

Excited by all this physical contact, the young girl was filled with a mad desire to offer herself entirely to her lover; Claude also could wait no longer; he arranged his friend across the bed and knelt on a cushion placed on the floor, having before his very eyes, and on a level with his lips, Claire's most secret charms. He paused for a moment to study the delicate grotto of love, completely wet in anticipation, framed by wispy blonde hair which started just above the sexual organ and extended upwards in a curly mass at the front. The sexual lips, pink and healthy, gracefully rimmed, provided the mount for her already swollen clitoris, the button of love. A delicate odour emanated from these secret organs; a natural odour in which was discreetly mingled the young girl's favourite perfume, white lilac.

Gently and very delicately, with the tip of his finger, Claude caressed these organs of love, covering them with tender kisses, arriving before long at the clitoris, which he left hooded for the moment; in order to prolong and intensify the pleasure as much as possible, he began to lick it with a short lapping motion using the end of his tongue.

The young girl, completely motionless, abandoned herself entirely to the waves of pleasure which broke over her; with closed eyes, cheeks tinged with crimson, stiffened nipples, her breath growing deeper and more irregular, she felt in the very depths of her being the extraordinarily exquisite and voluptuous sensations of this intimate kiss. Claude, without pausing for a moment, immediately flicked his tongue against her clitoris; he could tell from the involuntary movements of her legs that she was on the point of orgasm; now, in order to make it all the more intense, he parted the thin pink tissue which protected the button of love and continued to make the same practised motions with his tongue on the exposed clitoris itself, fully erect, while, very gently, he also inserted a finger in the narrow passage of her vagina which he moved back and forth in amorous combat.

Claire could take no more; an intense state of voluptuousness invaded her which made her entire being quiver; she screamed with pleasure, her body grew stiff, her thighs squeezed Claude's head in nervous reaction, and a hot liquid shot from her overstimulated vulva, for her lover had sought to continue his labour of love until the last possible second, so that the young man's face was now as wet as her own sex.

Claude quickly slipped away from her at that moment and, arranging his friend, who was by now in a swoon, on the bed once again, he now mounted her, gently forcing his erect member into the tiny opening of her vagina, which was wet with her own sexual juices. He leaned towards her and squeezed her in his arms. Claire came out of her swoon as this happened, and the voluptuous feelings that she had experienced a moment or two earlier had not dissipated themselves yet, as Claude, coming in his turn with tremendous rapidity, for that is how excited he was, inundated the inside of her sex with his burning sperm. They remained like that, intertwined in each other's arms, for a little while, mouth to mouth, eye to eye, savouring their happiness and their delight in possessing the power to give each other such sweet pleasures.

'Oh, my very own Claude! How I love you!'

'Clairette, how I adore you! The pleasure you give me is beyond comparison: I would like us to remain this way forever, intimately united, and to endlessly experience over and over the delirious intoxication I find in you.'

'My love, what pleasure you gave me! I am still shaking from the effects. Your tongue is so soft that I almost fainted with delight as you caressed me with it. My darling Claude, you will do this often to me, won't you?'

'Yes, Clairette, as often as you like, but it would be advisable for us to move apart now; I don't want you getting pregnant. If you like, I will help you wash your little pussy.'

After they had made their ablutions, they returned to bed and stroked each other tenderly.

'You called it my little pussy! What a pretty name for it. Do you like my little pussy, do you find it pretty?'

'Yes, my darling Clairette, I am head over heels in love with it. I think it is absolutely charming, and I hope to stroke it, caress it, and kiss it as often as possible; but above all I want to make it come as exquisitely as possible by giving it some nice little *minettes*.'

'Is that what you mean by a *minette*? The little stroking movements you give my pussy with your tongue?'

'Yes, darling, that is called to give *mimi*, to give a *minette*. In love, that is the thing which gives a woman the most intense orgasm. Those who have experienced it once, can never do without it again.'

'Oh, I believe you. Now I have experienced such intoxicating delights, I cannot imagine how I could possible do without. What a pity it is that you don't have your own little button of love, too; I would so enjoy learning to make you come in exactly the same way.'

'But Clairette, your pretty little tongue can give me exactly the same experience; you can give me *mimi*, only in a slightly different way.'

'But how is that possible? Oh, Claude darling, explain it to me! Teach me everything about love; I want to know everything; I would be so glad to make you feel what I felt a few moments ago.'

'Very well, since you are so curious, I will teach you the entire grammar of love, every rule and exception without omitting a single one; and, to begin with, I shall show you a charming position which allows two people to come at the same moment, while giving each other *mimi*. This position is called *soixante-neuf*, because of the similarity between the juxtaposition of the two numbers, and the way in which the two lovers have to place themselves, upside down, with regard to each other.'

Tenderly enlaced once again on the bed, Claude gently explained to his mistress what she had to do, and Claire tried to put into practice what she had learned. Sliding down to the young man's feet, with the tips of her fingers she stroked his thighs, stomach, his adorable testicles, and his member which began to grow stiff, discovering its crimson hood; then, summoning her courage, she pressed it to her lips, kissing it and stroking it with her tongue. Claude then pulled his friend towards him, so that she straddled him, but back to front, such that Claire was able to continue to caress him in this manner with her lips and tongue, while he, with his head between his mistress's thighs, had her pussy within reach of his mouth. They exchanged kisses. Claude began again to expertly lick her clitoris, which soon produced the desired effect: the hot-blooded girl once more felt the most voluptuous feelings invade her entire body, she wanted more than anything to make her lover feel the same pleasure, she licked his erection and took it in her mouth, sucking it passionately. His testicles contracted in her hand and suddenly a warm jet of sperm flooded between her lips, while she herself, having arrived at the paroxysm of pleasure, inundated Claude's face with her juices.

The two lovers, swooning as a result of the powerful climaxes they had just experienced, remained as they were for a few minutes; then, their spirits reviving, they wrapped their arms around each other and hugged each other madly; Claude was absolutely delighted to have found such an active and willing mistress, and Claire was overjoyed to have been able to feel all her lover's pleasure throbbing between her fingers and her lips. They lay like this, in amorous embrace, for some moments more, occasionally interrupting their kisses to whisper sweet nothings to each other, but day was approaching, and they soon had to take leave of each other, though not before promising to meet again in the same place.

During the course of the following nights, our two tender lovers did indeed come together many times. If Claire had in Claude one of the great experts in love, a man who was not only kind and tender, but also passionate, persuasive and inspiring, she was herself a most remarkably gifted pupil who required very few lessons to become acquainted with all the tricks of love, the different ways of offering oneself to one's lover, and the entire range of pleasures which constitute the exquisite art of love. One day Claude told her that the little hole hidden between her buttocks represented a serious rival to her pussy, its pink neighbour, and was quite capable of offering asylum to the virile member. Claire wanted to try out this new, and by no means uninteresting, method of making love, though not without a certain apprehension, it has to be said, for it seemed to her that the hole in her posterior was much too narrow to accommodate such an enormous engine.

Claude reassured her, promising her that the penetration of his rod in her narrow opening would be painless if the appropriate precautions were taken. He arranged her in the kneeling position on the bed, with

her legs apart, and the top of her body resting against a
pillow. In this manner her buttocks were wide open and
her tiny rosette was completely unprotected against the
combat to come. The young man caressed her pretty
bottom with the utmost tenderness, not forgetting the
top of her pussy, its greedy neighbour, which he licked
with his tongue, while he slowly introduced his index
finger to the little hole next door to feel how supple it
was; then he allowed his tongue to stray to the tiny anal
rosette, which he kissed in such a gentle manner that
such caresses are sometimes called 'rose leaves', because
that is how they feel. Completely impregnated with
saliva, the narrow orifice was ready to receive its new
guest. Claude, after inserting his member into Claire's
vagina and moving it back and forth a few times so as to
lubricate the skin, placed it against the narrow opening
of her anus and pushed the ruby-coloured head gently
into the tight tunnel, parting her buttocks slightly with
his hand in order to assist the process. Distending the
folds in this charming little orifice, the head of his penis
slipped in gently, and the young man, by applying a
constant pressure, without any sudden movements,
slowly managed to insert the full length of his rod
between the constricted walls of her anus. Penetration
was complete, and Claude had acted so tenderly that
the young girl had experienced no pain. Claire, for her
part, continued to stroke her clitoris with her right
hand, as Claude no longer provided this service for her,
and the strange sensation which she felt at having her
pretty arsehole impaled by the virile manhood of her

lover rendered her own orgasm, which her own hand had started to procure for her lower down, all the more violent. Claude was now moving back and forth steadily in his new retreat, his stiff erection squeezed by the warm and elastic walls of Claire's anus; soon an intense climax made him shake all over, while a copious ejaculation flooded his mistress with a warm liquid at the very same moment that she, climaxing herself, fell forward on the bed in a swoon.

Claire soon took to this new method of making love, which has the additional advantage of avoiding unwanted pregnancy, and on more than one occasion over the coming days she offered her lover this narrow passageway which, like its charming neighbour, leads to the most delectable of pleasures.

FEMALE LOVE

Claire knew all the refinements of love between a man and a woman; all that remained for her to discover was the love between women. Circumstances so arranged matters that the young girl was initiated into this final pleasure unbeknown to Claude and without her having any say in the matter.

The relationship that Claude had with Germaine, the pretty chambermaid, came to an abrupt end the day that he entered into complete possession of Claire. Naturally, Germaine was extremely upset at being abandoned in this manner and sought the reason for it. A young woman as cunning and as expert in the wiles of love-making as Germaine did not have to wait long before she was on the right track. She was well aware of the close intimacy which existed between the two young people, though she did not begin to suspect that matters could go any further between them given the young girl's natural reserve and chastity, about which she also knew. However, when Claude became Claire's lover, there was such a transformation in them, a joy so profound was painted on their faces, that it was impossible not to notice it. Germaine immediately buckled down to the task of verifying her suspicions, giving the lovers not a moment's grace as she spied on them in the house and in the gardens. As a result of all this poking and prying she eventually caught a glimpse of Claire slipping into Claude's bedroom from where she did not emerge until two hours later. From that moment she was convinced: Claire had given herself without reserve to the young man.

The possession of this secret gave Germaine control of the situation: a word from her, and Claude would be ignominiously chased from the château with hardly time to pack his bags. In this way she had the two lovers at her mercy. What use would she make of this information? Would she reclaim her lover? You would only believe that if you did not know Germaine with her lascivious instincts and her unconquerable penchant for other women. She had always been extremely attracted by Claire, whose charms and beauty she knew better than anyone as a consequence of her duties as chambermaid, and it was only because the young girl had met her timid advances with such hauteur and disdain that she had beaten a retreat and held her passions in check. But now the situation was reversed. Germaine summarised it to herself in these words: 'Now, young lady, it is you who is in my power!'

The very next morning she had to carry out one of the daily duties of her employment which consisted of looking after Claire as she got out of the bath – in other words, she helped her to dry herself and get dressed. When she had removed the wet chemise that Claire had worn during her bath, Germaine hesitated before bringing the young girl her peignoir while she contemplated her splendid nakedness, devouring with her eyes those firm, upright breasts with their crimson

points, the unsullied stomach, the dimpled thighs, and above all the triangle of blonde pubic hair which did little to hide the pretty little lips of her vagina. Claire looked at her maid with astonishment. At that moment the latter, giving way to an overwhelming sense of attraction, threw herself on Claire, cupping her breasts in one hand and murmuring words of passion as she slipped her other hand between her thighs.

Claire, furious at such disrespectful behaviour on the part of her maid, angrily shook herself free and pointed to the door. But Germaine told her what she had learned of her illicit adventures with Claude, wasting no words in explaining to her how she was now entirely at her mercy, that she had no choice but to submit to her passion, and that this was the price of her silence.

Claire was utterly astounded; a veritable look of anguish was written on her face. The young woman took pity on her, made her sit down next to her on a sofa, and rained kisses and words of love on her. She assured her that she would not have sought to blackmail her in this way except that she had to overcome her resistance at any price, so much did she desire her and, even as she wrapped her arms around her, she explained that nobody else whatsoever had the faintest inkling of her secret.

Germaine knew how to be persuasive, her very voice being sincerity itself; she rekindled a feeling of calm in Claire's spirit, who was already beginning to become strangely troubled and slightly aroused by the violence of the passion the young woman felt towards her. 'I love you,' said Germaine, 'I want to make love to you, and I want you to make love to me. I want you to experience the same things with me that Claude has made you feel.'

The young girl softened under this tempest of passion. Germaine laid her down naked on the sofa and kneeled beside her. She pressed her mouth against Claire's, kissing her passionately, sucking her tongue, and nuzzling her on the back of the neck in exactly the spot where the skin is the most sensitive and delicate. Next it was the turn of her breasts, which she caressed in the gentlest manner imaginable with her hands, before covering them with kisses; she sucked the erect nipples and teased them with the tip of her tongue, giving to these actions an extraordinarily sensuous quality. Her womanly fingers, as gentle as velvet, played with a surprising agility across the girl's ravishing body, brushing against her calves, stroking the inner part of the thighs, following the line of her stomach, before losing themselves in the little triangle of blonde hairs as she finally caressed the pretty lips of her vulva in the most exquisite manner. They brushed against her clitoris only to feel how erect it had become.

Claire quivered all over during these obsessive caresses for she was on the very verge of coming.

'Make me come, Germaine,' she cried out. 'Please, I want to come so much.'

But Germaine was not listening to her. She turned her over on the sofa in order to see her back and began to nibble the small of her neck. Then her agile fingers moved up and down along her spine in a caress of an exquisite gentleness; she started to massage the silky flesh of her buttocks, kneading them vigorously until they began to turn red. This licentious caress continued between her buttocks, concentrating on the perineum and the tiny wrinkled hole whose orifice was explored by a finger. This finger was quickly replaced by the tongue, which forced its way into the adorable hole. Still groping lower and lower, the velvety fingers explored the vulva, which was warm and damp under their touch, finally making their way to the clitoris which was throbbing with desire.

'Make me come,' begged Claire. 'I can't bear it any more!'

At those words, the young woman rolled Claire over so she was on her back again, lying diagonally across the sofa, while she herself knelt between her thighs and pressed her mouth against the burning vulva. This threw Claire into a state of ecstasy. The soubrette took the tiny lips expertly in her mouth and sucked them; her tongue penetrated into the depths of her vagina; finally, she caught the clitoris between her lips, rolling it, sucking it, teasing it with the tip of her tongue. Claire, breathless, shouted out in ecstasy, writhing with pleasure; a delirious spasm took hold of her, her vulva was full of her own ejaculation, the warm liquid running down her thighs and covering Germaine's entire face.

Claire tried to move away, but Germaine held her firmly in position.

'I want you to come again,' she said. 'And I want to really hear you this time.'

The young woman inserted one finger in her anus and another two in her vagina, such that the elastic sides squeezed together all around them; she alternately pushed them in deeper and deeper and slid them out, imitating the movement of the penis, and at the same time she ferociously attacked her vagina, which she continued to caress in her own ecstatic way for what seemed an eternity.

Claire was now literally screaming with pleasure, she came once, twice, three times, and each time the release was indescribable. Germaine had not been mistaken when she had said that she would make her experience an orgasm like never before.

As soon as she recovered her senses, the young girl expressed her heartfelt gratitude to Germaine for the intense pleasure she had given her. She took her in her arms and kissed her on the mouth, whispering words of love all the while. Germaine, excited to the highest degree, also had a mad desire to come; she looked the young girl in the eyes, in the most adoring way, and said in a low voice:

'I want to come so much, have you no pity for me?'

Claire blushed deeply, hesitatingly, taken by surprise by the idea of making another woman come, and did not reply.

'I beg you, my little Claire,' repeated the young woman, 'I really want to come! Give me your hand, that will do.'

But Claire, confused as she was, wanted to play her part.

'I will do better than that, and let you have my mouth.'

She then laid the maid on her back, rolled up her dress and underskirts, and opened the slit in her knickers as wide as it would go, gently nuzzling her little mouth into the young woman's mass of black pubic hair. She sucked, licked, nibbled, and made her tongue dart back and forth as best she could, throwing herself wholeheartedly into this new exercise for her, and so well did she do this that it was not long before she received full in the mouth the copious ejaculation of the young woman who was half-fainting in her arms.

Claire, whose appetite had been awakened by the intimate charms of Germaine, by her pretty pussy, shadowed by her thick black fleece and dimpled thighs, wanted to see her entirely naked. She undressed her in the twinkling of an eye, scattering at random her dress, petticoats, knickers, corset and chemise. When she was naked, she contemplated her with admiration, taking her ripe breasts in her hands, kneading her buttocks; while caressing her here and there, she seized her in her arms, pressing herself against her, mouth to mouth, breast to breast, pubis to pubis. The two women excited each other again to the point that they both wanted to come again, despite all the pleasures they had already given to each other.

An idea flashed across the lascivious mind of Germaine:

'Let us both come at the same time, that way we shall doubly enjoy ourselves.'

'Oh, yes! Let's do that!' said Claire.

'Do you know how to do it? Your Claude seems to have taught you such a lot already.'

Claire could not help blushing, but Germaine spared her further embarrassment by pushing her towards the divan where she arranged her on her back; she herself leaned over her, the other way round, and each woman pressed her mouth against the greedy sex of the other.

It is impossible to describe the nature of their orgasms except by pointing to the cries of ecstasy and the involuntary reflexes of the two delicious bodies which furiously wrapped themselves around each other, writhing with pleasure.

They only stopped when they were both absolutely exhausted, after having experienced all the paroxysms of orgasm, voluptuousness in its most delirious intensity.

CONCLUSION

Claire was too ardent by nature, too lively, too passionate not to engage subsequently in further voluptuous pastimes with her pretty chambermaid. She had herself become a great expert at pleasing her maid and nothing gave her greater delight than sending her into raptures by the artfulness of her touch. This feminine liaison, moreover, was a great consolation to the beautiful girl since it enabled her to endure a separation which, though expected – anticipated even – nonetheless occasioned her no little pain, and which occurred a few months later. Claude, her very own Claude, had to leave the château when he reached the age to be called up to do his military service. The two tender lovers took tearful leave of each other, promising that they would remain forever devoted to each other and meet again soon, whatever their respective situations, since a marriage between them was out of the question.

Claire felt the pain of this separation acutely; she was too under the sway of her voluptuous pleasures not to suffer when they were so brusquely withdrawn, and without the many kindnesses of her maid, she would hardly have known what to do with herself.

Less than a year later, the proprietor of a château in the region, who spent the greater part of the year in Paris, asked her to become his wife. Neither young nor handsome, the prospective bridegroom would by no means have been the first choice as a partner of a young girl who still had the fondest memories of Claude Larcher. But it was such a brilliant alliance that Claire had to give in to the demands of her family and agree to the marriage. The ceremony was quickly arranged and, thanks to the wise counsel of her good friend Germaine, and to a multitude of astringent lotions, it was not without some difficulty that the ageing Romeo garnered what he imagined to be the marriage hymen.

FIN